7/17

This book should be returned to any branch of the
Lancashire County Library on or before the date shown

Lancashire County Library,
County Hall Complex,
1st floor Christ Church Precinct,
Preston, PR1 8XJ

www.lancashire.gov.uk/libraries

LL1(A)

Also By Claire Hennessy

Nothing Tastes as Good

LIKE OTHER GIRLS

CLAIRE HENNESSY

HOT
KEY
BOOKS

First published in Great Britain in 2017 by
HOT KEY BOOKS
80–81 Wimpole St, London W1G 9RE
www.hotkeybooks.com

A CIP catalogue record for this book is available from the British Library.

ISBN: 978-1-4714-0634-8
also available as an ebook

1

This book is typeset using Atomik ePublisher
Printed and bound by Clays Ltd, St Ives Plc

Hot Key Books is an imprint of Bonnier Zaffre Ltd,
a Bonnier Publishing company
www.bonnierpublishing.com

Week zero, day four

I am surrounded by idiots.

'. . . it's thirty quid but it's seriously, like, the best foundation ever, swear to God . . .'

'. . . did you see her latest video? The eyelash tutorial is amazing . . .'

'. . . I need to figure out what I'm doing with my hair for Friday . . .'

These are the dyed-hair, perfect-make-up girls, a brigade that get up an hour earlier in the morning to look beautiful even though no one can possibly look remotely attractive in the St Agnes's school uniform. You can roll up that regulation-length maroon skirt at the waist to show off your legs but it doesn't change the fact that it is a hideous monstrosity. And who are they trying to impress, anyway? It's an all-girls school and I bet the closest any of them have come to queerness is one of those showing-off-for-the-boys kisses.

'I can't believe she gave me a B, it's just because she hates me. It totally deserved an A.'

'I know, she's so harsh, it's not fair.'

To the other side of me, the braniacs are bemoaning the

grades on a history project we just got back, which I'd have a little bit more sympathy with if this was an exam year and not Transition Year, dossiest of doss years. Also it just feels off, karmically, to ever admit out loud you think you were entitled to a better mark.

I am a groupless, friendless creature in a sea of chat. As soon as I push past the world's slowest walkers to get through the door of our assembly hall, I search for somewhere safe to sit. Front row, far left – a teacher's pet location but also means I don't need to watch everyone else drifting in. In pairs, in threes, in gaggles.

I don't need to avoid eye contact with Steph, is what I really mean.

Phrases float towards me as the hall fills up. What a vlogger posted this morning, who's going to get kicked off some reality show, what a teacher said yesterday.

My fingers itch for my phone, safely stowed in my schoolbag, to access something that matters. There's this case in the UK I'm following at the moment, this girl whose uncle raped her but the judge said she led him on and was very mature for her age. Sure, you know what thirteen year olds are like.

This is the world we live in and I'm sitting in a hall with a hundred girls who sort of . . . haven't even noticed?

And I know that whole thing of going 'I'm not like all the other girls' is super-problematic because, hey, what's wrong with being a girl, and can't we all move past gender stereotypes, and all that shit, but if you went to St Agnes's, you'd understand. Land of the girly-girls, trapped in the 1950s, like something out of Enid Blyton except less cuddly.

Actually, maybe not even like Enid Blyton, because Darrell Rivers kicked ass. (I may re-read the *Malory Towers* books every Christmas. Shut up.)

'Ladies!' Mrs O'Connor trills from the front of the stage. 'Settle down, please!'

We settle down. Mostly. There are some girls at the back still yapping, who are treated to one of those sour-lemon frowns until they shut up.

'We're going to have a very important day today, so I hope you all take full advantage of it,' she starts, and I tune out, because we have had many of these Very Important Days so far this year – and we're only halfway through November. Basically everything else gets cancelled for the day and we go off to some local historical site or have someone come in to talk to us about mindfulness. Today has been billed as a 'retreat', which we all know from two years ago is code for sex ed.

'. . . smaller groups, and then your facilitator will lead you through the activities . . . I'd ask you to make sure you give them your full attention . . .'

Mrs O'Connor likes speeches. Speeches and Catholicism. Her two favourite things.

'Remember you're representing the school today, ladies . . . spiritual ethos . . . meditation . . .'

I snap to attention. Spiritual what?

It's an actual religious retreat. For fuck's sake. I'll be lucky if I don't burst into flames.

We are sitting in a circle on the floor of a darkened classroom,

3

eyes closed. Allegedly closed. There's a lot of eye-communication happening. Across from me, new girl Felicity – a Blyton school-story name if ever there was one – is smirking at the other cool girls, while Steph engages in some surreptitious phone-checking.

'You're on a beautiful beach,' the lady at the top of the room intones. 'Just take a moment to see it. Feel the warmth of the sun on your face. Feel the sand beneath your toes. Listen to the waves gently lapping against the shore.'

Just when I think it couldn't get any worse she starts making wave sounds, her own eyes shut and her hands moving in time with the air hissing from between her teeth.

A muffled snort comes from somewhere else in the room. Ann-Marie, our saintly class prefect, purses her lips.

'Now we're going to travel a little bit further down the beach,' the mad woman continues. 'And in the distance you see a small wooden hut . . .'

Guess who's in the hut. Go on. Guess.

Yes, ladies and gentlemen, boys and girls, and all the genderqueer and non-binary humans out there, it is the one, the only . . . Jesus!

'What do you want to ask him? Think about that for a moment, and then when you're ready, ask. He's ready to listen.'

The only spiritual thing popping into my head right now is *The Book of Mormon* soundtrack, which I'm pretty sure is not what she has in mind.

It goes on in this vein. After break time, crayons – yes, crayons – are passed around and we are invited to draw our image of God.

4

'There are no right answers. This is a chance for you to reflect on your own personal view of God . . .'

I blame Enid Blyton for this, really. I thought a girls' secondary school would be all jolly japes and tricks on the teachers and passionate friendships and faintly queer overtones. When my parents gave me the choice between the two nearest schools to us – St Agnes's on one side, the less-well-thought-of mixed-sex school on the other – I listened to my heart and not my head. I bet they don't have to do God-art in Greenpark College.

Twenty minutes later we are invited to share and discuss our personal views of God, and by 'invited' I mean 'forced', which seems a bit dodgy if it's supposed to be a personal thing. We get through five old-white-guys-with-beards and two clouds-with-smiley-faces before it's my turn.

I hold up a blank page. 'Um. I don't really . . . have one.'

A head shakes in disappointment. 'Would you like to tell us a bit . . .'

'No,' I say tightly. 'Move on.'

A little bit of a gasp from someone – probably Ann-Marie – but no one says anything. More beards. A wise elephant from Felicity. The door swings open and Mrs O'Connor leans in the doorway, listening in. 'How are you getting on, ladies?'

No response at first, then a muted chorus of 'fine'.

She stays, waiting.

'Who do we have next?' our lunatic leader says.

Steph looks up. 'Pass.'

I am conscious of Mrs O'Connor stepping closer, actually going around the desks to look at the pictures.

'Let's see what you have,' the lady persists.

'Pass.' It comes off more insolent than I think is meant, but what the hell do I know any more?

'Just show it to the group, Stephanie,' Mrs O'Connor snaps.

Steph holds up the oversize sheet of paper. Even from a distance I can see it is not an image of God so much as a comic strip. I make out some of it and realise: it's us. It's today. And I am betting it is not a kind take on us.

Mrs O'Connor takes it. A moment of silence, and then everything is cold. 'Stephanie. This is absolutely disgraceful. Please take this to the principal's office.'

Yep. Typical St Agnes's logic: bring in someone to tell us there are no right answers but punish people for not giving them anyway. I am mid eye-roll when Mrs O'Connor spots it, and stalks across to my desk. 'And this is yours, Lauren? Nothing? Not even bothering?'

We are not each other's favourite people. You'd never guess.

'You can join your friend in the principal's office,' she barks, and then turns around to face the others. 'I hope the rest of you are behaving yourselves and treating today with the respect it deserves.'

I'm sure there's more to her speech but Steph and I are out of there, our offending artworks in hand. The principal's office is only down the corridor, and I tell the secretary that Mrs O'Connor sent us.

'Wait here,' she says after some tut-tutting. 'I'll see if Mrs Carroll is available.'

Steph slides into the seat next to me. 'Just like old times.' Said lightly, but carrying more than it seems.

I know what I am supposed to do. Grin and agree, complain

about how ridiculous this all is. In another life I would have. That's how you behave around your best friend.

Instead I stare at the comic strip and go, in what I am aware is a snotty tone, 'Actually, I think that's really immature of you.'

It's the first overtly mean thing I've ever said to Steph and I know it is crossing a line. I can feel it in the air. But it means less than it would have before the summer. So. So I don't care. Not really. I don't.

The principal's door opens and we are beckoned in.

'Lauren,' Mum says, sighing. 'What is it now?'

Week zero, day six

'And she made us both apologise for, like, not having the right idea about God, and to that absolute *wagon* Mrs O'Connor because she's the one who organises these things, and . . . ugh. My own mother.'

I wait for Justin to say something, to be equally outraged by this, but he just kisses me.

Oh. Okay. Kissing is good. Kissing is nice. I am a girl with needs. Except.

'I just really wish she'd –' I don't know. I wish she'd stop being such a principled principal, maybe. She only took over this year but she's made this big deal of how she has to treat me the same as every other student, a speech delivered first back in August and then repeated at dinner time after our retreat. 'It's just –'

'Just what?' He waits. And then kisses me again. His hands go to my breasts, underneath my T-shirt.

(I feel like a body. Not Lauren. Just a girl-body to be touched.)

'Can you listen to me for two fucking seconds? I'm not a sex toy.' It comes out louder and angrier than I intended. There is something flaring inside me, hot and raw.

'What the fuck? Come on, you came over here, we've, like, twenty minutes before my parents get home . . .'

(He's right, he's right, I'm a terrible person.)

(Wait, since when did going over to your boyfriend's house constitute a binding contract about shenanigans?)

I stare at him. Spiky blond hair. Blue eyes. A boy who usually looks at me with admiration rather than irritation. A boy who is suddenly, unexpectedly, making me want to scream and cry.

'I should go,' I mumble.

'Don't be like that.'

'I'm not – *you're* being –' I can't finish the sentence. My throat is all blocked up.

I don't start crying until I'm at the bus stop, which is just a tad mortifying.

I want humans. I want kindness. I want my hair stroked and I want to be told I'm okay, I'm right, I'm not a horrible monster.

I pull out my phone.

'Oooh, you're such a *girl*,' Ellie mocks, passing me the open bottle of red wine. We are drinking from the bottle because we are epically classy, oh yeah.

'I know! I know!' My voice is more high pitched than usual, which is part upset and part alcohol. 'All the feelings! All of them! But like, hi Justin, can you remember that I am an actual person and not just a vagina?'

She pats my head. A few of the girls across the room – the trio of Posh Pansexuals – look over at the mention of the word 'vagina' and then go back to their conversation.

'And wanting to talk about something that's bothering me

9

with my boyfriend – why does that make me a bad person? How am I the bad guy here? And he's like, oh, we're running out of sex time.'

More head-patting.

'But now I feel like the crazy one. Like, how is that fair? Why is the girl always the crazy bitch even if the guy's being a dick?'

'I know, I know,' Ellie soothes. 'It's nearly like we live in some kind of patriarchy.'

'Fucking patriarchy,' I mutter.

'Fucking patriarchy!' she yells, which prompts everyone else to join in.

Sometimes I love Q Club and our crazy rantings about how shit the world is. This is where to go for feminist rantings or getting to talk about the messed-up-ness of being presumed straight until proven otherwise. These are my people.

'I should break up with Justin,' I say. 'He's too normal.'

'He *is* a straight white dude,' Ellie agrees.

'Straight, white, cis, able-bodied dude,' I amend.

'Straight, white, cis, able-bodied, *middle-class* dude.'

'The most oppressed of us all,' I say.

We snort, and drink more wine.

Everything's okay here. Everything is okay at this party I was planning to skip in order to go have sex with my boyfriend, which on reflection makes me a terrible feminist and I should hang my head in shame. In shame. Q Club is where my friends are. My real friends.

Then Steph comes back inside after having a cigarette with Marc and I remember the bits of Q Club I am less crazy about.

Like Marc.

Marc with a c. If you're going to go to all the trouble of picking a new name after you come out as trans, at least pick Mark with a k. For fuck's sake. The world of manly, masculine, macho names open to you and you pick Marc with a c.

And, like, if you're deliberately going for something not super-macho then why the need to take testosterone and to talk about it all the time? Dude, we get it, T is The Best Thing Ever, let's move on.

I am pretty sure no one would be that enthusiastic about oestrogen. Like, Ellie doesn't go on about how much she wants to take lady-hormones. Pronouns and clothes a bit more feminine than you might expect (today, slinky purple T-shirt with skinny jeans) and that's it and it's not a big deal.

Who the hell would want lady-hormones, anyway?

I don't realise I've said this aloud until Ellie says, 'Time of the month, pet?'

'Fuck off,' I say. Not in a mean way.

'Aunt Flo come to visit?'

'Stop.'

'Vampire tea party?'

'Gross.'

She holds up the bottle of wine to the light. 'It's the right colour, anyway.'

I grab it off her. 'I'll text you the second it arrives. All the gory details. Number of tampons used . . .' I wait for this to be too much, then continue. 'Blood clots . . .'

Ellie puts her hands over her ears. 'Stop it.'

'I win!' I do a little victory dance from where we're sprawled on the couch, and catch Steph's eye. Not impressed.

11

Well, sorry for reminding you that you do actually have lady bits, Steph.

John, our host, brings in more popcorn from the kitchen. He's just gone eighteen, properly out and proud and mad camp, even at school (he's at the same school as Justin and even their year Know) but I still remember the first Q Club meeting he was at, all nervous and quiet and shy.

You get over that pretty quickly.

'How's it going, Lauren?' John asks, joining me and Ellie on the couch.

'Grand,' I say.

'Liar,' Ellie says.

'Stupid boyfriend,' I amend.

'Boys are stupid,' he agrees. 'Can't live with them, can't live without them.'

'Yeah,' I say sadly.

'Get more drink into this one,' John instructs Ellie. 'Oooh, how about shots?'

'Oooh, shots,' Ellie says.

'No. Shots are death,' I say. This is based on exactly one experience over the summer, after exams finished, at another Q Club party, but I will stand behind this decision for at least . . . until college, maybe.

'Shots are life!' John corrects. 'Live a little, darling.'

'*So* gay,' I say.

He smirks and kisses me on the cheek.

I sink into the couch, taking another swig from the wine bottle. It's going to be okay. Everything's going to be okay.

I watch Steph and Marc together, heads close, in intense

conversation that the rest of us aren't privy to.

Maybe shots.

Messages to Justin sent at some point after Ellie, John and I finished another bottle of wine but before I fell asleep in John's little sister's room:

I just wish you would try to understand what it's like when someone treats you like that and doesn't even listen to you or take your feelings seriously.

Oh of course you don't care why do I even bother?

Maybe a blow-up doll would be better for you?

YOU ARE THE PATRIARCHY.

SO DONE WITH YOU.

Week zero, day seven

'Shots are evil,' I groan in Ellie's general direction as I stumble into the sitting room.

'Unnnngh,' she responds, raising her head from the couch slightly.

My mouth tastes like dead things. And my phone scares the shit out of me. At least I didn't message Steph. But did I say anything? The end of the night is blurry.

'I am never drinking again,' I declare.

'Whatever you say,' she says sleepily. I tousle her hair – kept short, she's not out at school yet – and rummage around for my coat in the pile on the armchair.

John emerges from the kitchen as I'm about to open the front door. 'See ya, Lauren,' he says with far too much cheeriness for this hour of the morning. I make some kind of mumble in response, and he laughs.

As soon as I've left the house, out comes my phone. Justin doesn't answer the first three times I call, so I send a message – *Sorry, stupid & drunk last night! xxx* – and wait.

I will not be the crazy stalker who calls ten million times. It's not even noon yet. He's probably still asleep, or maybe he

14

lost his phone, or has it switched off, or something.

Except I *feel* like the crazy stalker on the bus heading back home, slipping my phone in and out of my bag every two seconds to check if there's a reply. And then just as I'm getting off, a beep. It's like the sun coming out.

We r goin in2 town 2 do sum shopping want 2 come?

Just Dad. Dad, who is still coming to terms with owning a smartphone and a data plan that doesn't necessitate using old-school text-speak.

My body is a toxic wasteground. No way am I hanging out with the parents looking at exciting saucepans or whatever it is they have planned.

No thanks, enjoy yourselves! x

I will crawl into bed and consider my life choices and then Justin will call. I contemplate sending him another message saying that the parents are out of the house for the next while, if he wants to come over, but then rethink it. I don't want it to feel like I'm bribing him with sex, making up for our missed opportunity yesterday. Plus I feel too disgusting to really be up to it right now.

I kick my shoes off and crawl into bed, my phone left charging on my bedside locker, my laptop on the pillow next to me. I get *Frozen* going, which, yes, is a kids' movie but is also amazing – Idina Menzel! Kristen Bell! Love and frozen hearts! – and half watch, half snooze.

Musicals are soothing. So I'm all zen, or at least something approaching it, but then the phone rings and it's Justin and there's a boa constrictor crushing the life out of me. 'Hi,' I say warily.

'Hi,' he says. Similar tone.

'Sorry sorry sorry,' I say in a rush. 'I just went to this party and we were talking bullshit and drinking and . . .'

He waits.

It's not quite like a dagger straight to my heart but it's not far off it.

'Honey, I'm sorry, I didn't mean it, I was just – annoyed. And sad.'

'*You* decided to walk out,' he reminds me.

'I know.'

'And you made me feel terrible for just wanting to be with my girlfriend.'

'I *know*.'

'It just came out of nowhere. Like, I'm not psychic.' His voice gets louder on that last word. I can hear the pain and it kills me.

'I'm sorry,' I repeat, tears springing up again. I am a one-woman sobbing machine. I know if I could see him right now it'd be different. Doing this over the phone, without physical contact and context, is too sad.

'If you don't want to be with me –' he begins, and white noise takes over.

Buzzing. And fear. My heart. My pounding, terrified heart.

'I do. Honey. Justin. I do. I'm crazy about you.'

Please don't break up with me, please, please, please.

'But, come on, Laur, you made it sound like I'm a monster or something.'

'I'm *sorry*, okay? I was with some friends and kinda worked up and we were drinking . . .' I swallow. I can't say anything

16

else without hysterical sobbing, and I hate how I feel right now, and I just want this to be over.

Silence on the other end.

I wait. I wait. And then I hang up.

I have *Frozen* on repeat. Every single bit of it hurts, even the funny bits. Even the fucking dancing snowman is ripping at my heart. The sounds coming out of me are howls, like something inhuman.

My phone is off. Dealing with people seems too hard. I've deleted my Facebook account – no big deal, I can always reactivate it, but the thought of logging in and seeing that Justin Maguire is no longer 'in a relationship' is horrendous. (Do they really need to have that picture of a broken heart turn up when someone changes their status? Isn't it a bit too on-the-nose?)

I don't even know what I want. I'm angry with him and want him and I just want him to get it, to get that I was stupid and drunk but also that I was really upset, and doesn't that count for anything?

It's like feeling anything too much makes you crazy. Crazy girl! Which is extra shit because Justin once said that the thing that impressed him about me, first off, was that I was passionate and opinionated. That I was strong. (I'd never thought of myself as strong before.)

We met over the summer. At summer camp, actually. Not the American kind you read about that are set in the woods and have cabins and pranks and sailing and lanyard-making. Not even overnight, unlike this mad nerdy thing that Ellie does every year where you get to live on a college campus and take classes and apparently it's – her words – 'gloriously fucking weird'. This was a two-week programme at an arts centre near where Mum used to work, before she decided that her absolute calling was St Agnes's.

It was this songwriting thing. Steph was maybe going to go, before everything changed, and I said it to a couple of people from Q Club who were all 'maybe, maybe' and never got around to signing up. But my parents are big believers in Keeping Me Occupied for the summer and anyway, I wanted to be there. But as soon as I got there, the fear kicked in.

The particular kind of fear and inadequacy that hits you in certain situations. Like, I played violin for a couple of years in primary school and gave it up because it was too hard, but also because there was this other girl in my class who was just a proper genius at it. She'd been playing since she was three or something ridiculous like that, and there's nothing more depressing than being ten years old and already feeling like you've missed your shot at being a prodigy.

Same thing again here, surrounded by all these cool people – I was suddenly so terrified they were all going to say they'd already produced loads of material and recorded it for YouTube and it'd got ten million hits and they were going on TV the following week, actually.

And then I saw this guy. And our eyes met across a crowded room.

And he looked so incredibly too-cool-for-school that immediately the anxiety gave way to rage. I wanted to say, 'Why are you even here?' I mean, language classes or extra maths or whatever is one thing – exam-related, totally the kind of thing your parents would force you into. But songwriting? Who the hell ends up there and then makes a point of looking bored?

I decided I wasn't going to bother with him, which goes to show that sometimes the whole you-can't-trust-first-impressions, *Pride-and-Prejudice* thing is right, after all.

Mum and Dad insist on parading their purchases: new cushions for the living room, and a pair of shoes each, half price! I try to look interested and vaguely cheerful, and then we sit down and watch some TV before the weekly Skype call to Brian and Liz in Australia. Brian's my brother – twenty-eight, does something with computers, don't ask me what. Liz, the wife – also Irish, even though he met her out there. They both do this thing where they act more Irish than anyone here actually does, now that they've living abroad. Case in point:

'Say hello to Granny and Granddad, Caoilfhionn!' Liz says, holding their eighteen-month-old on her lap and making her wave. Oh yes, they're spelling it that way. Any sensible person living – well, anywhere – would opt for Keelin so that the poor child doesn't spend the rest of her life having to pronounce it for everyone, but hey, national pride. Or something.

Mum and Dad dissolve into doting-grandparent mode. 'Helloooooo, hellooooo,' they coo at the screen. 'Who's a pretty girl? Who's a pretty girl?'

This goes on for a few minutes. I smile and wave at the screen too – I mean, she is cute, but there's only so much of this a rational human can take.

Brian comes on. 'Heya,' he says, looking tanned and healthy.

It's breakfast time there, we can see what I'm pretty sure is freshly squeezed orange juice behind them.

'How's it going, pet?' Mum asks, and we listen to stories about work and surfing and what Caoilfhionn's been up to lately. I start to zone out. It's all so adult, so otherworldly, and I keep thinking of my phone upstairs and whether if I turn it back on there'll be a message from Justin, and if there is, what I'd do with it.

'How's school, Laur?' he asks finally, and I offer up a smile.

'It's fine.' Well, what else am I supposed to say with the principal sitting next to me on the couch? The woman whose office I was sent to this week?

'Anything exciting coming up?'

'School play, a couple of trips . . . you know yourself.' Standard Transition Year fare, no matter what school you're in. Brian's school did *Oklahoma!* with the girls' school down the road, and had at least three trips to the local park when the teachers couldn't think of anything else to keep them busy during their non-exam year.

'D'you know what play yet?'

I shrug. 'No idea.' I turn to Mum, half kidding. 'Mum won't tell me.'

'I can't tell you,' she snaps. 'Stop pestering me.'

My mouth opens and closes. I stare at the floor, at the hole in one of my socks, right at the big toe.

'How's the new school?' Brian asks, even though he's asked her this in previous weeks.

I wasn't *pestering*. I asked once, maybe a month ago, if she knew. That was it. And it's okay if she doesn't want to tell me,

20

or feels she can't, or whatever. It just feels like I'm in trouble, in a way that I didn't know I could be. Like I am somehow a bad daughter.

I can't look at the screen again until Caoilfhionn comes back on, Liz making her wave bye-bye at us, and then I hide in my room for the rest of the night.

Week one, day one

Sunday morning. Stabbing pains of doom. Wetness between my thighs. Sheets . . . I lift up and check – yep. Blood, blood, blood.

How can something that happens once a month still be such a fucking disaster every time it attacks?

In the shower, letting hot water pound over my belly and then at the lower part of my back, it hits me: oh, fuck, Ellie was right. Time of the month. Stupid lady-hormones.

How do I even know what I'm really angry about when everything hurts? Is it always going to be like this – never being quite sure whether it's okay to be annoyed or whether you really are just, well, a crazy girl?

Before

'This is so shit,' you say.

'So shit,' I agree.

'So incredibly shit. I want to rip my womb out with a –'

'Spatula,' I suggest.

You burst out laughing. 'Do you even know what a spatula is?'

'No,' I say, laughing as well.

'You'd need a knife or – ooh, one of those cake slicey things!' Your face lights up in that way it does when you have a plan.

'Okay, I'll go get one. Get ready!'

You lie down on the couch, arms at your side, eyes closed.

For a second I forget the twisting agony, the fact that I'm rushing to the bathroom every few minutes to make sure I'm not bleeding through onto my jeans. For a second all I can see is you.

And then it passes, and I return brandishing a cake knife, intoning solemnly, 'Just relax, this won't hurt a bit . . . it'll hurt a lot, though.'

'Laur,' you say, but in a way that lets me know it's really a compliment, 'you're actually deranged.'

Week one, day five

Teen magazines lie. They lie about many things, but especially how much blood you lose in an average period, because there is no way this is just 'a couple of tablespoons'. Unless they actually mean giant spoons the size of proper tables.

They also lie about the benefits of 'gentle exercise'. Case in point: PE this week, which made me throw up afterwards. (In the bathroom. Not on the actual basketball court, which would have been extra gross, and also prompted the super-competitive sportsy types to make sneery faces at me.)

Now I am staring at my phone trying to find the appropriate words to explain how cramps so bad they make you want to puke can mean you're not quite up for apologising to your poor misunderstood boyfriend, and just how exhausting the whole damn thing is.

Hey honey, I'm really sorry about the crazy. Bleedy time of doom & pain & much insanity. I miss you. L xxx

I amend 'bleedy' to 'hormonal' to minimise the grossness, and then get annoyed with myself and change it back. So what if Justin goes 'ew' a little bit? He's not the one with a mother who believes in going into school unless someone (preferably yourself) has actually died or if a limb is missing. He's not the one who's spent the last five days in agony, with at least a day more of this to eagerly anticipate. Fuck him.

No, self. Stop listening to your crazy-lady hormones. This is how you got in trouble in the first place, and one of us has to break the stalemate. Suck it up. Play nice. I swap it back to 'hormonal' and add another 'really' before the 'sorry'.

Okay. Send.

Ten minutes later the phone is ringing. 'Hey, you,' I say, hoping it is good news.

'Hey,' he says, and I can almost see him from the way it sounds, all slouchy and sexy.

'Hey,' I echo.

'Hey.'

We crack up.

The relief, the relief, the relief. It races through my veins. Or maybe that's just the heavy-duty painkillers talking.

'So,' he says, 'my parents are going out on Sunday . . .'

'Sunday, you say.'

'Sunday.'

'Okay.'

Can't sleep. Online. (I should get that printed on a T-shirt.) Ellie's really good at finding the weirdest stuff online and sharing it, so I watch a video of something that starts off as a boy-band parody and ends up turning into a superhero story, and read a blog about how to decorate your wheelchair before I get back to what other friends have posted.

John is moaning about exams – this is his last year of school so the pressure is on – and one of the Posh Pansexuals is name-dropping Z-list celebrities that her parents know. I keep scrolling.

Literally had a panic attack yesterday before PE. Changing rooms = no. CANNOT FUCKING DO THIS.

Oh, Steph. My heart twitches in my chest, even though a tiny bubble of annoyance is manifesting at the same time. Like getting changed for PE is fun for anyone. It has always been its own special kind of torture. But. But.

Message: *Heya, sorry about being snarky at you after Retreatgate. Hope you're okay. x*

It's the first message I've sent since the 'thanks for letting me know' over the summer. I deliberately don't scroll back up.

Week two, day one

There is a frantic bird flapping against my ribcage as I wait outside Justin's house. What if he's still annoyed with me a bit? What if I've misread this and we're going to have a serious talk about the state of our relationship because he thinks that's what I want the whole time? (I would like sex today, please. I deliberately refrained from self-pleasuring in the shower this morning. So there.)

He opens the door. My eyes meet his.

When he kisses me, fireworks go off.

The first time we had sex: awkward, clumsy, non-orgasmic (for either of us, so at least that's fair). My house, over the summer, right before school started again, loud music on even though we were alone there and also because just-sex noises seemed like they might get a bit ridiculous.

This time: he's a little bit more impatient than usual. Not forceful, just – you can see in his eyes how much he wants this. Those blue eyes. His hand between my legs and then he's thrusting in sooner than I'd like, and it's not like I'm not wet or anything, it doesn't *hurt*, but I know that after he comes this way we're going to watch stuff on his laptop or something, not worry about getting me off.

Before Justin I always thought that you'd have to demand equal-orgasm-opportunity, like it was all being added up on a balance sheet, but in real life it doesn't work that way.

I can get myself off but this – Justin's hair matted with sweat, his eyes wide and adoring, the closeness of him – is something beyond. A safety, a happiness.

We manage another round before his parents get home.

Week two, day two

Walking to school, I listen and sing along to 'I Don't Like Mondays', 'Monday Monday' and 'Manic Monday'. If I was a hipster type I'd listen ironically to these songs on, say, a Friday, but it actually is Monday morning and I would much rather be crawling into bed with Justin than trudging into St Agnes's.

Steph and I once looked up St Agnes. Virgin martyr. Patron saint of chastity. A tiny smirk comes to my face, remembering that. And remembering yesterday.

I am waiting for the traffic lights to change when I realise there's another girl in uniform next to me. Next to me as I sing along and have a stupid smile on my face.

'Hi,' Felicity says, offering up a tiny smile.

I can't tell if it's a bitch-smile or not, which maybe sounds paranoid but if you knew the girls she was hanging out with, you'd understand. So I just nod and then stare at the ground until the green man appears. Once we're across the road, I pretend I need to pause to check my phone so she can go on ahead.

When I get to the school gates, there's a gang of them – from my year and the two years above – all chatting and yapping and huddled together and basically somehow managing to leave only a sliver of space in a gateway wide enough for cars and buses to get through.

Normal-human etiquette: be aware that other people exist and that you might be blocking the way.

Cool-girl etiquette: ignore the fact that there's a girl with a large schoolbag on her back trying to get past.

'Excuse me,' I say, and am ignored.

'Excuse me,' I say again.

And then, 'Would you mind getting out of my fucking way?'

Which sounds harsh but is actually the only thing that works. I stomp past, hearing the giggles and less-than-subtle murmurs behind me.

Mum's car is already in its usual place, just outside the main entrance. She's always in wildly early, otherwise I'd be getting a lift with her. I'll take the walk over an extra hour and a half of time hanging around this place. For a second I imagine dropping into her office and commenting on girls hanging around at the gate and not letting people through, being inconsiderate and rude – not because it's making my morning crap, of course, but because it might 'reflect poorly on the school'.

Fortunately for them I am not that unbearable a human. I go to my first class instead, Literature and Culture with the gorgeous Ms Lynch. Seeing her walk into the room is a bit like I imagine taking a Xanax might be – instant reassurance. She is like the kind of teacher you get in heartwarming movies, the ones who don't just follow the rules and do the bare minimum but who make jokes and notice stuff and put their whole heart into the job. Last year she ran an after-school bookclub – which

30

was basically just me, Steph and a handful of babies from First Year, but you have to admire someone who stays so positive even in a school full of girls who just don't give a shit.

'Morning,' she says. 'God, Mondays are dire, aren't they?'

Sometimes I think I want to be her when I grow up and then other times I think I just have a bit of a crush on her. It's a fine line.

'What are we doing today, Miss?' Ann-Marie asks politely. Or at least it sounds polite, but is a tactic she uses to make herself look super-dedicated while also sort of testing the teachers to see how prepared they are.

'I thought we'd do some chemistry experiments,' Ms Lynch replies, total deadpan.

I snort.

'Okay! We don't have our full class this morning as there's an assembly scheduled, but this week we'll be looking at the fantasy genre.'

'What, like *Harry Potter*?' someone says, sounding as if that is just so desperately uncool she might die.

'Ah, girls, come on, tell me you know enough about books not to think J. K. Rowling invented fantasy. Throw out some other authors for me.'

Silence. Not because no one can think of anything, although some of them are probably too stupid to have ever opened a book outside of school in their lives, but because daring to be anything other than completely bored is just *so* pathetic. Ugh.

'Tolkien.' That's me.

'Neil Gaiman.' Steph.

'Terry Pratchett.'

31

'Ursula Le Guin.'

'George R. R. Martin,' another voice offers up. I look back. Felicity.

'Yes, *Game of Thrones*, girls! I know loads of you watch it.' Ms Lynch surveys the room. 'Fantasy. Worlds of magic. Dragons. Elves. Witches. Goblins. All that kind of stuff. So what do we think of it?'

Again silence. Then Ann-Marie says, 'It's a bit childish, isn't it?'

Ms Lynch's face lights up, like she's been waiting for someone to say this. 'Brilliant. That's a very common idea, Ann-Marie, and what we're going to be looking at this week is why that's not true.'

Only Ms Lynch could sound this genuinely cheerful and passionate while telling our beloved class prefect that she's wrong. I'm dying for more, but that's when the intercom crackles and we are told to go to the assembly hall.

'How are things, Lauren?' she asks as we fall into step together, which would be mortifying if it was any other teacher but instead is just a tad cringy.

'Okay,' I say.

'Such enthusiasm! Well, there's some good news coming now.'

'How good?'

She laughs.

It clicks for me. 'Are you telling us which play we're doing this year?'

She grins, says nothing. Which is a yes. You'd think Mum might have given me the tiniest bit of a heads-up.

'Fill up the rows at the front, ladies!' My least-favourite teacher is directing when we go through the doors. I try to slide into the row behind but Mrs O'Connor calls me back and insists I take the last available spot in the previous one, next to – oh. Steph.

I offer up a tiny smile. Get a tiny one back in return.

Mrs O'Connor and Ms Lynch take the stage. Devil, angel. Voldemort, Harry Potter. No, wait, she'd be Lupin.

'What?' Steph says.

'What?'

'You just whispered, "no, wait, she'd be Lupin" to yourself.'

My face heats up. I am officially losing my mind. 'Ms Lynch,' I say.

'Oh, totally.' This is said with complete genuine agreement, because it does make sense if you know the series. A wave of missing-Steph slams into me.

I'm about to say something else – what, I don't know, just something to keep this fragile moment going – when the microphone is tapped.

'Thank you for coming, ladies,' Mrs O'Connor says, like we had a choice in the matter. 'Myself and Miss Lynch here have some news for you.'

For a split second the phrasing makes it sound like they're about to announce their engagement, and the mental image is terrifying. Then I hear the 'Miss' and watch Ms Lynch's face go just a tiny bit hard, and for, oh, about the ten-billionth time since coming to this school, I want to punch Mrs O'Connor in her smug face.

'As you know,' Ms Lynch says, 'every year the TY girls put

on a production for the rest of the school and your doting relatives. Gives them an excuse to get out of the house and tell you how great you are.'

Mrs O'Connor neither likes nor appreciates the humour, I notice. Well, tough. This is always Ms Lynch's baby.

'This year, as Mr Kelly's retired, Mrs O'Connor has very graciously volunteered to co-direct . . .'

Of course, the universe is not on my side right now. I watch Ms Lynch's face, listen carefully to the words. 'Graciously volunteered' means she stomped her way into it, insisted on it. Mr Kelly was always the helper, none of this co-directing business.

Ann-Marie puts her hand up ever-so-politely and asks, 'Are you able to tell us yet which show we'll be doing?'

'Well,' Mrs O'Connor says, clasping her hands together, 'we can indeed. Can't we, Miss Lynch?'

Ms Lynch says, 'Of course we can, Carmel.'

Oh, I do love her.

'Stop swooning,' Steph whispers in my ear.

Carmel chooses to ignore the informality – or maybe insolence? She loves that word, I happen to know – and says brightly, 'It's a lovely show called *The Boy Friend*.'

What the actual –

'Eh, what the –' someone murmurs behind me.

'Is that a play?'

'Don't have a fucking clue.'

'I really need to get my hair cut, these split ends are a disaster.'

Someone off to the left pulls out her phone, but I can't tell if she's searching for the title online or just checking her messages.

I have never heard of this thing, so it must be a play, which means no singing, which is a slap in the face. Except through the buzz around me I hear Ms Lynch saying it's a 'classic musical'.

As the owner of a large collection of musical soundtracks – on actual CDs, not just downloads – I beg to differ with this assessment. *The Sound of Music. West Side Story. The King and I. Mary Poppins. Singing in the Rain. Evita. The Phantom of the Opera. Les Misérables.* These are classic musicals.

I know hoping for something like *Wicked* or *Spring Awakening* or *Hamilton* would be ridiculous, but you'd think they'd pick something people had, well, heard of.

'D'you think there'll be any decent boys?' someone says.

'Boys our age? Are you kidding me?'

'Oh my God, my boyfriend is such a good singer.'

'Yeah, but the face on him.'

'Ladies!' Mrs O'Connor chastises, silencing the hum.

A hand in the air. 'We just want to know which boys' school we're doing this with.'

I know the answer before it's given. Somewhere in the distant past there were co-productions with a boys' school a mile away. But no more.

Mrs O'Connor frowns. 'Don't be silly, Valerie, it's a school play. A St Agnes's production.'

See what I mean? I think about how *Wicked* would make so much more sense with an all-female cast – how many musicals actually have two female leads? Meanwhile, there's groaning and mumbling and sighing and gasping from the audience.

'You're not serious, Mrs O'Connor,' the poor deluded Valerie continues.

Her face goes tight. 'Ladies, this is *school tradition*. This is how it's been every year.'

Felicity puts up her hand, surprisingly. 'Isn't this Mrs Carroll's first year as principal? Maybe if we asked her . . .'

I can feel my face heating up.

'It's not Mrs Carroll's decision,' Mrs O'Connor says sharply.

'But if it's school tradition, then . . .' You can tell she's a new girl when she's daring to keep up the argument, not understanding how pointless it is.

'That's enough.' She does her death-glare. 'Felicity, I'll speak to you after assembly.'

A little 'oooh!' noise goes around, which sets off Ol' Carmel even more. 'Ladies! You're not small children any more!'

'Then why do you treat us like we are?' Steph and I mutter under our breaths in unison, then exchange a grin. I'd feel better about this if we hadn't been given such crap news.

'Anyway,' Ms Lynch says. 'We'll have auditions next week, and we'll be putting on the show at the end of February or else early March – we'll have exact dates for you closer to the time. Any more questions?'

Don't do it, don't do it, don't do it. But Steph's hand is going into the air, and I can feel the kinship of the last few minutes dissolve. 'So basically you want half the year to be in drag?'

I know the detention's coming before I hear it. Insolence. What Carmel O'Connor calls it every time someone says something she doesn't like.

I know Steph is waiting for me to commiserate. But all I can think is: how could you not see that coming, you idiot?

Week two, day three

I am supposed to be discussing how fantasy can be used as a way of exploring social issues, but since I'm in a group with vapid morons this is not happening.

'Like maybe racism?' someone with bleached-to-death hair says.

'Yeah, that's good,' someone else says vaguely.

In another corner of the classroom, Steph uses the word 'problematic' and it is both endearing and irritating to hear it.

I cannot believe we are doing a crap musical. It keeps hitting me. I can't believe Ms Lynch thought this was going to be good news for me, as though she doesn't know me at all. The roles you practise in front of the mirror (oh come on, we all do it) are the ones like Maria, Eponine, Christine, Elphaba. Not Polly Browne, heroine of *The Boy Friend*, who attends a finishing school in France (I *wish* I was making this up) and meets a boy and falls in love with him and there are misunderstandings but then it's all okay and that's it. That is literally the story.

'Okay, what do you have so far?' Ms Lynch asks, appearing from behind the blond idiots.

There is silence in our group. A silence that I would normally fill.

I cross my arms and refuse to meet her gaze.

'Lauren?' she says.

I shrug, without looking up.

Doesn't she *get* it? She's supposed to be one of the things that make this place better. Not worse.

Yes, I am sulking.

So. Fucking. What.

I'm thinking about him. In a sappy way.

'You just – go for it,' Justin said to me back in that songwriting camp. This was the third day, I think, the Wednesday of the first week, and we'd been put into groups of three to write a parody of some pop song. I can't even remember which one it was but you know the kind, all I-love-you-baby and then getting borderline-stalkerishly *problematic*, but still really catchy. And it was silly and fun and I loved it.

I'd been watching him, Mr Spiky Blond Pretentious Hair looking too-cool-for-school as the two girls he'd been put with actually worked. They were whispering and giggling and scribbling, heads together over a copybook, while he was distant, doing his own thing. Writing whatever in his Moleskine notebook of pretentiousness. He didn't join in when they performed, or rather spoke, their song, and I wanted to punch him.

'Lauren, Sarah, Mariam, you're up next!'

And we actually got up, stood up and threw ourselves into it, belting out the alternate lyrics – we really played up the stalker elements, and people were properly laughing with not at it, which is always such a buzz.

We were the last group to go, and then we had our coffee break, or fizzy-drink break really, and that's when he said it to me. Mr Spiky Blond Pretentious Hair said to me, 'You just – go for it.'

I was all ready to snap at him that going for it is sort of the point, that he was wasting his time by not participating (and yes, *yes*, of course I'd have sounded more like Mum than I'd like by saying that), when I looked at him and realised two things. One, he had beautiful blue eyes, properly piercingly gorgeous ones like you'd see on TV except probably helped along by coloured contacts. Two, he wasn't being a dick. He was saying it in an impressed way.

My mouth opened but I had absolutely no idea what to say. 'Oh,' I finally said, like an idiot, and even though it sounds too neat to be true, a little part of me knew even then that something would happen between us.

So I need him. I need him, is what hits me, in my chest and in my gut. I need Justin to . . . this sounds so pathetic, but I need his arms around me. I need a dose of being taken-care-of, to be cuddled up to him.

And, yes, okay, all that other stuff too. But mainly a distraction from this, from school, from disappointment.

I take out my phone underneath the desk while we're up in one of the computer labs. The teacher's paying attention to the third of the class struggling with Excel spreadsheets and praising the couple of girls working on some coding project, and ignoring the rest of us reading or watching stuff online.

I contemplate just turning up at his house, surprise surprise, but that seems more creepy than romantic, and anyway I want to double-check there'll be no one at home. His parents work late and both his sisters are usually out with either friends or at after-school study. So I message first, and the reply comes in speedily.

See you then! xxx

Justin gets very free and easy with the Xs when there's sex on the way.

As soon as the last bell goes, I race to my locker and then to the bathroom nearest the sports pitch. It's the one place where you can change out of your uniform and leave school by the nearby door without passing reception or the teachers' car park, where the more pathetic teachers like to lurk and send people back inside to change. We're not allowed to be on school grounds out of uniform, not even change into runners to walk home.

In here, you can tell who's heading off to meet a boyfriend (or maybe a girlfriend, to be fair, but I just don't get that vibe from any of them), because they're at the mirrors doing their make-up while the girls staying for after-school sports mutter darkly about their space being invaded.

I duck into one of the stalls. Do not need to be accused of perving on the girls changing in front of the mirrors, totally carefree about their bodies. Also do not need to feel bad about my body around those of them that are freaks of nature and beautiful enough to post selfies on Instagram without filters.

Out of uniform. Razor out to quickly de-stubble legs (am I

just weirdly hairy or does everyone's leg hair race back to the surface of their skin about two seconds after they get rid of it?), and then deodorant. Into jeans, top, shoes and spare knickers kept in locker just in case, at least since the start of this school year, now that I have a boyfriend to skip off to see. Make-up applied while I balance a tiny mirror on the toilet cistern.

I step out into a mist of hair spray, coughing slightly.

'Sorry!' It's Felicity, blond hair bouncing on her shoulders.

'It's okay,' I say, automatically. The way you do even when it is clearly not.

She's in this gorgeous red dress, casual but clearly on her way to meet someone, and – don't look at her, Lauren, for fuck's *sake*, someone will have told her you like girls and she'll think you're being an Evil Lesbian Predator. (Which now that I say it sounds like it should be a superhero movie, one I would totally go see.)

'I'm going to see my boyfriend,' I say, and as soon as the words are out of my mouth I feel like an idiot.

She gives me a weird look. 'Okay. Uh – have a good time.'

And then I feel defensive, so I add, 'Just in case you thought I was checking you out. So, you know. Get over yourself.'

SHUT UP LAUREN OH MY GOD.

My face has never been this hot in my entire life. I may spontaneously combust.

So I shove past her and a couple of the older girls out into the corridor, where I feel like the air's a little cleaner and I can breathe, and then I stride out the side entrance.

I am a disaster of a girl.

Week two, days four to seven

It's like some giant invisible hand has turned on a tap. I can't stop thinking about sex. I go home from Justin's that day, still thinking about his lit-up face and unbuttoning his less-hideous-than-mine school shirt, and take the kind of long shower that leaves no hot water for anyone else in the house. My dreams turn erotic – not always about Justin, sometimes weird amalgamations of people that are half celebrity and half someone you know.

We wrangle two more afternoons before the weekend, and swap messages in between: the kind adults tell you not to send. Not pictures, just words, until Justin sends a dick pic and I look at it not really knowing what to do with it.

It's not that I find penises repulsive, it's just that it's all out of context. I'm pretty sure he doesn't want me to send a photo of my lady bits. I have to think about it a bit before it does anything for me: imagine him stroking himself until he gets hard and then getting his phone ready to capture the moment. Then I have something honest to message back: *Pic making me type with one hand here . . . xx*

It keeps me giddy and cheerful, all of this. On Saturday both sets of parents are home so we go to the cinema and paw at each other and end up doing it in the disabled bathroom, which would usually make me feel guilty but I didn't see anyone in a wheelchair and anyway if someone knocks we could get out.

Having sex while standing up – well, sort of half standing, half leaning – is maybe not as super-satisfying as it looks in movies, but it feels daring and passionate. Once we're finished, and the used condom is safely wrapped up in toilet paper and in the bin, we leave and I'm pretty sure we look smug as hell and also that it's incredibly obvious what we've been doing.

And I can't bring myself to care.

Before

'Laur?'

'Yeah?'

'I think I like Katie.'

'Katie from Home Ec?'

'Yeah,' you say, sighing.

'Super-straight Katie from Home Ec?'

You groan, burying your head in the pillow. 'I know! Why? What's wrong with me?'

'You've crap taste in girls,' I say.

'Not helping,' you mutter.

'Aw, pet, I'm sorry,' I say, really meaning it. I put my arm around your waist, hold on to you like you're a tiny child and I'm protecting you from something. You're smaller than me, anyway. Like a pixie.

You snuggle in closer. 'I'm doomed,' you say.

'You're not doomed.'

I can feel you breathing. In, out. Your chest rises and falls. There is something both safe and dangerous here.

'You wanna go to Q Club this weekend?' you ask suddenly.

'In town?'

'Yeah. It's supposed to be really good.'

'Meh.' The idea of a support group just seems a bit cringy. I imagine everyone sitting around in a circle. 'Hi, my name is Steph and I'm so gay,' I say, pretending to be you. 'I'm here to get over super-straight Katie from my Home Ec class.'

'Shut up, you'd love it. You'd make friends with all the gay boys and talk about musicals.'

'And what are you going to do, find gay girls to listen to Melissa Etheridge with?'

'Tegan and Sara, you sap.'

'Or, like, half the pop stars out there are now bi, apparently.'

'Attention-seekers,' you say, and you know damn well that'll make me tickle you until you shriek, 'Okay, okay, stop!'

'Say it.'

'Labels are for clothes, not for people,' you sing-song. 'Except you're so totally gay, Laur.'

'I've never even kissed a girl,' I point out.

You know what I'm hoping for, right? There in your bedroom where we're hanging out on a lazy Saturday afternoon, with no one interrupting us, with the world far away, I'm telling you I've never even kissed a girl and that's the moment you need to shrug and go, 'Well, we can sort that out.' You should be lifting your head from the pillow, letting your eyes meet mine, and then moving your face closer and closer until I can hardly breathe, until your hand is gently tilting my chin up and your lips touch mine.

My whole body fizzes in hope and anticipation. I can see the script. Why can't you?

'So what?' you say. 'I've never kissed Katie but I know I want to.'

Katie from Home Ec – quiet, pretty, uneventful – has never done anything to me. Ever.

But right now she seems like the worst person in the world, and I hate her.

Week three, day one

While my parents are at Mass – thankfully they haven't expected me to attend since I was thirteen – I scroll through the Q Club group chat on my phone.

Ellie: *Hey who's going to the thing in the National Gallery today?*

Sandra: *What thing?*

John: *Have to study.*

John: *Kill me now.*

John: *If one of you do it they can't say it was a hate crime.*

Steph: *Not funny, dude.*

Ugh. I have a message half typed about how it actually was kinda funny, and if you can't make those jokes in that chat then where can you, but I delete it.

I close the chat, wondering if the buzzes that indicate new messages coming in are Steph emphasising this point and lecturing everyone, or if it's just Ellie trying to persuade people to go to this exhibition and art workshop.

It sounded interesting when she messaged us about it a few weeks back, but now . . .

Okay. So. So even though Justin has a family thing today,

he might be finished by the afternoon and then we could hang out, and there's no way I can make that a thing that fits with these guys.

You don't bring your super-straight super-cis boyfriend to a Q Club thing, you just don't.

(Is it pathetic to be skipping something just in case your boyfriend is available? Ugh. Don't answer that.)

I decide to be productive instead, and do more investigation into this wretched musical. We don't get to audition for specific parts – just audition for a 'main' part if we're interested – but I've already realised that playing the simpering Polly Browne with her too-predictable love story might corrode my soul.

After some YouTube research, by which time the parental units have returned from their weekly pray-fest, I decide it has to be Maisie – her best friend, and the fun one. She reminds me a bit of Glinda in *Wicked* – not the one you relate to the most but the one who gets more laughs, who is funnier and brighter than the actual lead.

One of the bland, *nice* girls can be Polly. Ann-Marie, or Imelda O'Connor, Mrs O'Connor's niece – the kind of girls who ooze faux-wholesomeness. I'll be the flirtatious, mischievous one. Cool girl, not crazy girl.

I sing 'Won't you Charleston with me?' at the mirror.

'Lauren?'

'Yeah?'

Mum opens the door. 'You singing?'

'Yep.'

'Homework done?'

'Yep.' It's a light homework year. She should know that.

'So you're auditioning tomorrow?'

'Maybe.' I shrug. Yes. Yes, *obviously* your musical-obsessed daughter is auditioning, even if it's not the greatest choice of title. But then again you didn't tell her anything about it, so . . .

'Good luck,' she says. 'I mean, break a leg.'

I offer up a little smile, and then she leaves, and suddenly my nose and throat are all prickly.

It's not like I approve of nepotism but Imelda O'Connor is almost certainly going to get a really good part, and meanwhile my own mother is so determined to be fair that she won't even listen to my rants about good ol' Carmel or anything school-related any more.

I reach for the phone. No word from Justin. Just more messages piling up in the group chat. I imagine Ellie and the Posh Pansexuals (Sandra among them) hanging out in the gallery, or wherever they've gone to afterwards. I imagine Steph and Marc glued together in their so-special-no-one-else-gets-us way that they have. And then I turn back to the mirror and start singing again.

Week three, day two

Somehow I imagine it'll be like it is on TV: walking out on stage solo, a panel of judges sitting in the audience making notes, a polite 'thank you' when you're done. Instead, we're in one of the music classrooms, where one of the girls from the school orchestra sits at a piano.

Somehow I thought we wouldn't be watched by everyone else. I know it sounds stupid when you're auditioning to perform in front of an audience, but my throat feels too tight knowing I'll have to sing in front of all the other girls here.

I perch on one of the desks, my feet swinging.

'Hey,' a voice says to my right. Felicity pushes herself up onto the adjacent desk. Smiles a little.

'Hey,' I echo, and the epic cringefest is flooding back now. *Get over yourself.* Ugh. I have to say something.

'I –' I start, but am interrupted by – of course – Mrs O'Connor.

'Right, ladies! Can I have everyone standing, please, no sitting on the tables.' She makes it sound like a mortal sin. Adultery, murder, sitting *on* and not *at* a desk.

The first thing we do is have to all sing together, while Mrs O'Connor and Ms Lynch walk around listening to us, having eye-conversations. I try to ignore them and just sing, trying to imagine myself on stage doing this. Imagine myself in costume, in a pretty dress instead of a scratchy maroon jumper with the school crest on it. I am cute and mischievous in an old-timey sort of way. I live my life through song and dance.

Ms Lynch smiles at me, and I realise I'm dancing on the spot, imitating a routine I watched online.

I can do this. I can be one of the leads. I can be Maisie. Or even, if they offer it to me, the over-the-top headmistress. I can be *good* at this.

'No need for the dance routine yet,' Mrs O'Connor says, smiling in an entirely different way.

And just like that the bubble's burst. She's drawn attention to it, and now I'm a schoolgirl again, with my face turning hot. I am aware of Felicity to my right, of everyone in this room who is prettier and cooler than me. (It sounds so stupid when I put it like that, but that's how it feels. That they're better. They've received some sort of manual for how to be a girl that never arrived in my letterbox.)

If I ever become a teacher – which everyone thinks I will because of Mum (yet they weirdly never assume I'll be an accountant like Dad, helloooo sexism) – I'd want to be the Enid Blyton type, where they might be strict but are never cruel, or if they are cruel they've had their comeuppance by the last chapter. Or maybe one with twinkling eyes that everyone loves. Oh, or Miss Honey from Roald Dahl's *Matilda* (there's another decent musical we could have done) – kind and understanding and gentle.

If Mrs O'Connor has ever read *Matilda* I bet she rooted for the Trunchbull.

'Okay, ladies.' She claps her hands together. 'We'll listen to you individually now. In alphabetical order . . . so we're starting with Ann-Marie Bolger.'

Up goes Ann-Marie. She's not the best. She's not the worst. Ciara Byrne is next, and then . . .

'Lauren Carroll.'

I step up beside the piano. Heart pounding. I clear my throat. And then I sing. A little shaky on the first line, but then I realise I'm doing it, I'm actually doing it, it's okay. It's better than okay.

'Thank you,' Mrs O'Connor says when I'm finished, a little tartly, I think, but I'm buzzing now. I want to keep singing. I remember this feeling from songwriting camp – the nerves and then the adrenaline kicking in. The thrill of performing.

Ms Lynch gives me another of her lovely smiles, and I have *almost* forgiven her for making us do such an old-fashioned musical.

'You're really good,' Felicity whispers to me when I go back to my place.

I know I'm supposed to say 'No, I'm not', be properly modest and self-deprecatory, but I'm on a high. 'Thanks,' I mouth back, and grin.

And suddenly it feels less awkward with her, too. We've survived a moment of weirdness and come through it.

This is the power of music. It makes you realise things. It makes you put stuff in perspective. It makes you stronger. More – I hate this word, and my mum loves it – 'resilient'.

52

If I get this – if I get to sing and dance in school this year – St Agnes's might not actually be the worst place in the universe. It might actually be one of those 'best days of your life' moments after all.

Week three, day three

'They're letting us know tomorrow, which means they've probably already decided most people by now. Oh God. I think it was okay, it felt good, you know? But Mrs O'Connor still has it in for me so who knows?'

'Laur,' Justin says.

'So Imelda's probably going to be Polly and then I bet Katie's going to be Tony, they're the main leads, and then there's Maisie and Bobby, and . . .'

'*Lauren.*'

I pull my coat around me tighter. 'What?'

'Can we not talk about the play any more?'

'It's a musical,' I say. And then, 'Fine. What do you want to talk about?'

He shrugs.

There are tears edging their way into my eyes. 'No, go on. You've basically just told me to shut up, so you pick something else.'

'I didn't mean – you've just been going on about it.'

I didn't realise saying a few sentences about a thing that is important to me equalled 'going on about it'. I cross my arms tightly, trying to keep myself steady. Afraid to say anything else. How did our lovely walk through the park become this? It's crisp but not freezing, and the sky is clear and navy, and it's almost December, almost Christmas, and it was feeling almost winter-wonderland-ish.

Except I suppose it wasn't.

'How was school?' I say, trying to be cheery and good-natured. It makes me feel like a housewife in a 1950s sitcom. *How was your day, honey?*

'Fine.'

Silence. Heart thumping in my chest. Not like during the audition. This is bigger and scarier. We're teetering. I don't like this. Already the annoyance is fading and I just want this to stop.

'Go on,' he says finally. 'Tell me more about your musical, you future superstar.'

Relief. Like a giant wave swooping in and clearing the beach of any debris, leaving only smooth, golden sand behind.

Week three, day four

Yet another Important Assembly. Only this one genuinely feels like it. There's a buzz of excitement – maybe not shared by everyone, but enough of one to lift this out of the ordinary.

I remember Justin telling me, 'You just go for it'. And, 'You future superstar'.

There is also a voice in my head wondering if boys just offer up compliments to keep you on side so they can sleep with you. Maybe I'm deluded. Not talented at all. Not good enough. Shouldn't have even bothered auditioning.

Ms Lynch and Mrs O'Connor take the stage and the *wanting* hits me hard. I want to be on stage singing and dancing and performing, the rush and the thrill of it. I want it so badly I am suddenly sure no one else here could possibly have this same deep-in-the-belly yearning. Not these girls with their obsession with hairstyles and vloggers and skinny lattes. Unthinkable.

'We're delighted to announce that the part of Polly Browne will go to . . . Imelda O'Connor!' Mrs O'Connor says, trying to look neutral and as though this isn't a big fix. Imelda, who is sort of pale and quiet, gets a round of applause and smiles in a way that doesn't quite seem to fit with the situation.

She knew already, I realise.

I find Ann-Marie in the row behind me, fiddling with the gold cross around her neck – one of the very few items allowed under our uniform code. Is it nerves or impatience?

Ms Lynch announces that Polly's suitor, Tony, will be played by Ann-Marie.

With a sickening, heavy stomach I start to understand that this is the formal announcement of something that's already been decided. Everyone with a main part has already got a heads-up.

I stare at my shoes – black and scuffed, Mum is always reminding me to polish them – as the rest of the cast is announced. Felicity has been cast as the slightly bonkers headmistress, Madame Dubonnet. A dainty, spritely creature I don't know terribly well, Tara, is picked for Maisie. I'm sure she's lovely. I'm sure I don't really want to hit her over the head with something heavy.

More out of habit than anything else, I look for Steph in the crowd. Head down. Ignoring all of this. Until the chorus groups. 'Perfect Young Ladies,' Mrs O'Connor announces with a beam, leaving us with absolutely no doubt which the best group is. These are the finishing school girls – the ones fluttering around Polly and Maisie, being even more vapid and absurd. I listen to the names called out, the real-life ditzes. And then. Steph.

What's Carmel playing at? Seriously? I look over but there is no eye contact made, no opportunity to exchange what-the-fuck expressions.

They don't get around to calling my name until they get to who's going to be in the male chorus groups. Oh yes. I am to be one of the gentlemen who appear every so often to do things like remind the girls how great they are. I am part of the crowd and too – too what, too tall, too bulky? – too *something* to be one of the girls.

I cannot burst into tears, despite the mountain-sized lump in my throat. I can't let anyone know how much this hurts. I sit through the breathless 'omigod, *congratulations!*' whispers to the real cast members as the teachers say a few more things about rehearsal times, and then I escape to the bathroom furthest away from the hall and slam the cubicle door shut behind me.

I hate this place.

At lunch time, I take out my phone to message Justin, but the words won't come. I don't want him to know that I have to play a boy. It feels weird. Like it will make him interrogate his relationship with me, and wonder if it's because my legs are too hairy or if my jaw is too square.

This is what happens when you don't spend all your time researching how to do your make-up in such a way that makes you look beautiful but also makes you look sufficiently 'natural' so you won't be marched down to the nearest sink to wash it all off. If you want to be believed as a girl on stage, that's what you need to do.

This is not the kind of thing Justin would understand, or want to.

I open up the Q Club group chat, scrolling quickly through all the messages I've missed, and then type: *Hey everyone! Anyone around this afternoon? Need to get AWAY from school. xx*

It's a long shot. But maybe John will be fed up with exam-cramming classes and want to vanish for a few hours.

58

Maybe one of the Posh Pansexuals will be up for skipping school and listening to a rant about how terribly backwards St Agnes's is, in this day and age, over coffee. Maybe Ellie – nah, Ellie is too much of a nerd. Going into school hungover, grand, but actually leaving school in the middle of the day? No way.

Steph: *Me too. See you @ gate in 5?*

I weigh up the options before having an oh-screw-it moment. Because today is definitely an oh-screw-it kind of day.

Before

This is like it is in the movies. Bad girl influencing the good girl. You hold up the bottle triumphantly, a wicked grin on your face. 'Refreshments,' you say.

I half expect a montage to start up: girls knocking back drinks, laughing, dancing, making funny faces, running through the streets having adventures. All to a peppy soundtrack – that old 'Girls Just Want to Have Fun' song maybe.

Instead we take decorous sips of the wine from actual wine glasses – but not the good ones. Geraldine would freak out if we went near her collection of Waterford Crystal. Or pretty much anything else she owns.

I'm glad she's not here tonight. I'm glad she has no idea that the girly sleepover her daughter's having might not be all that innocent.

'What d'ya think of John?' you ask.

'From today?' Our first Q Club meeting, after two false starts – when we went all the way into town and then got giddily nervous and ended up wandering around the shops instead.

'Yeah,' you say, taking another dainty sip. I am jealous of how sophisticated you look, how adult.

'He seems nice. Kinda shy.' But I get that. Once we were in there, we were chatty – but it's easy when you have a friend with you.

'I bet he's freaking out over nothing. He seems totally straight. He'll end up married with, like, ten billion children.'

'He might be bi,' I remind you. 'Or pan. Or . . .'

'You just want everyone to be bi,' you say.

'I do not! I don't even like the word.' I have been thinking about this a lot. It sounds like you need to have two partners on the go at all times to satisfy your needs. (My current number of partners: zero.)

'Okay,' you say. A slight pause. The kind where I know that something's coming. 'But, like, *bi* the way . . .'

I reach for a cushion to hit you with. You shriek, and hit back, and we're giggly and silly and then we drink more wine and watch this movie about a girl sent to a gay rehab camp. (And 'camp' is appropriate, it's all pink and blue and ridiculous. But in a knowing sort of way.)

'Wait, is she your one from *Orange is the New Black*?' I ask.

You check your phone. 'Yeah. She looks so young. This came out ages ago.'

'Came out,' I echo, and we both dissolve into laughter.

'Lesbi honest here,' you start.

'Sapphic . . . tional story,' I bat back.

Your face is scrunched up. 'Aaaagh, I can't think of any others!'

'It's like . . . Ellen on earth?' I try.

You wince. 'DeGeneres or Page? No, I don't want to know, that was dire.'

The cushion comes out again to whack you over the head.

And then there's that moment. On the screen, it's the big damn kiss between the two female leads, and we sit in silence. The air is prickling. My skin is about to leap off my bones. 'Whoa, yeah!' you cheer, raising a fist in triumph.

I think your response is maybe a second too slow. Maybe to break the tension. But I don't know. I don't know if I can trust my instincts.

Do you ever think about me in that way at all?

Week three, day four

It is not a big deal to walk out through the school gates during lunch time. We're allowed out for lunch, allowed to race home if you live nearby, or down to the chipper or Chinese takeaway if you don't. The big deal is not turning up for afternoon roll call, but that's for Future Lauren to worry about.

'My house? Mum's at work,' Steph suggests.

'Or into town?' I say hopefully. Neutral territory. Not ready to be in Steph's room just yet, and I realise with a pang that it's probably gone through a makeover since the summer.

'Sure,' Steph says, maybe getting it, maybe not. 'Just let me get changed out of this first.'

This being our gloriously hideous uniform. I have flashbacks to late-night blog posts at the end of August: *Told that I have to wear a skirt because it's part of the school uniform, no exceptions. This fucking school.*

I had to skim over those, seeing how Mum was on the other side of it, explaining patiently that the regulations at the moment were very clear and that because it's an all-girls school it's not discrimination if you don't have a trousers option and that even if she wanted to change the rules she'd need to talk

63

to the board of management first . . . (all overheard, of course, like she'd ever tell me anything directly these days).

'You could pretend you're Scottish,' I suggest now.

Steph looks at me with one of those are-you-on-drugs looks I remember and miss from before this summer. Before.

'You know, like it's a kilt,' I add.

'I could. But, Laur, there's something very important you've forgotten.'

'What?'

'This skirt is fucking grotesque,' Steph says solemnly.

I laugh. Properly laugh.

'How about I play the bagpipes to distract from the grotesqueness?' I say.

'You'd have to play them really badly.'

'I'm pretty sure that's the only way I could play them.'

And we're giddy again, like things used to be, like the last few months of weirdness are falling away.

As soon as Steph's ready – jeans and an oversized checked shirt – I immediately feel too prim and proper in my uniform. I think about the spare set of clothes in my locker at school, or my wardrobe at home, and then I sigh and get over it.

We go wait for the bus, which, despite the app insisting will arrive in two minutes, actually takes fifteen, and listen to music, one earpiece each. Heads together. Like the old days.

There are so many things I want to ask but all that stuff feels distant now, abstract, safely locked up in words shared on screens and not anything that we need to address today.

'I don't want to be a Perfect Young Lady,' Steph says when

we get onto the bus, going for our usual seat – second from the back on the top deck.

For a second I think, yeah, me neither, but then I remember it's actually the name of the chorus group and not what we're supposed to be at school. (Though really it's both, isn't it?)

'It's not really you,' I say, which is the understatement of the year.

'Yeah. I think there's *prancing* involved.'

'I should expect so, dahling. How very becoming.'

A gentle nudge, and a head on my shoulder. 'Shut up, it's going to be shit. It's only 'cause I'm short.'

'You are a pipsqueak,' I agree.

'Shut up.'

'No, *you* shut up.'

We are still giggly and 'no you!'-ing each other when the bus deposits us in the city centre.

'So, I have to be a boy,' I say when we sit down for coffee (well, hot chocolate). I feel super-sell-out-y that we're in a Starbucks, but there are ten bajillion of them around and there's space to sit, alongside a whole bunch of hipster types writing their screenplays or whatever it is they're doing. (Dad would say, 'Have they no homes to go to?')

'Lauren,' Steph says seriously, 'you don't have to jump on the bandwagon. Just because loads of people in Q Club are trans or non-binary, doesn't mean . . .'

I pale. 'No, I mean –' Fuck. Here we go. Here it is.

Steph's head goes to the table. Head in hands. Shaking shoulders. What have I done now? Have I missed the latest

Being Super-Inclusive And Respectful Update? Is it even *okay* for me not to want to dress up as a boy for the musical or is it horribly offensive?

And then – 'Oh, you *brat*.'

Steph is not crying. Steph is cracking up.

'I meant the musical,' I say with dignity.

'I think –' There's more, but it's not coming out through the laughter. 'I think – you might be misunderstanding – what – what –'

I scowl. Okay, faux-scowl. 'Oh, go on. I patiently await your wit.' I cross my arms.

Steph takes a moment. Does that passing-hand-over-face thing that actors do to get into character. 'I think you might have got the wrong idea about what Transition Year is all about.' Then dissolves into laughter again.

'Oh my God, how long have you been waiting to use that one?' I say. Also I want to steal it except I know I can't. Shouldn't. Whatever.

'Too long. Way too long.'

'Anyway,' I say, to get back on track, 'the musical.'

'Ugh. I know. It's so stupid. Did you audition?'

'Yeah.' But then I quickly add, 'But I wasn't really expecting to get anything. C'mon, Mrs O'Connor hates me.'

My attempt at saving face meets Steph's sceptical face. 'Yeah, but you're a good singer. She should've given you a decent part.'

'Well, darling Imelda needed to get the lead, obviously,' I say.

'But of course! Never mind that she's the world's worst human being.'

'Is she?' I've never really paid much attention to her. But I suppose she *is* related to Carmel.

'She was in my science class last year and every chance she got she went on about how the *natural* family unit was so important. I think she's in one of those mad religious groups, or her parents are, anyway.' Steph's face scrunches up.

'That's such bullshit.'

'Eh, maybe she's right. I was raised by a single mother and look how I turned out.' Steph grins.

I know it's supposed to be a joke but I can't join in. Before I would've said something like 'Yeah, you freak', but now it's like . . . we're not on the same playing field any more. Steph is officially More Oppressed than me, or something.

'Ah, you turned out okay.' Polite. Bland. What you might say to an acquaintance, not a friend. I slurp up the rest of my hot chocolate. 'You ready to go?'

We wander through the George's Street Arcade, pawing at vintage clothes and second-hand books and contemplating getting nose piercings. Then into Temple Bar, where the cobblestoned streets would be easier to walk on if I wasn't still wearing my school shoes. Despite the weather being crap – it's started drizzling – there's still gangs of tourists around here, listening to some busker doing cheesy old Irish folk stuff. Steph and I step around them, do more wandering. Like old times, except now we look at different sections of the clothes shops. Which strikes me as silly, because there's nothing particularly girly about the rail of trousers in this shop, it's not like they're covered in flowers or vaginas or anything. Is there extra crotch space in men's trousers? Is Steph going to stuff it with a sock the way eleven-year-old girls stuff their bras? I edge over to the men's section and surreptitiously start feeling them, but stop when a guy comes over because, yes, I know this looks weird.

In my bag, my phone starts buzzing. Mum. Fuck. I thought I'd make it through until she got home from work. Stupid, because work is school, my school. I ignore it. A minute later I get the beep that lets me know there's a voice mail. Joy.

'D'you want to go to the cinema?' I ask.

'And where were you this afternoon?' is the first thing Mum says to me when I walk through the door that evening.

'Town.' Might as well be honest.

She does her stern-principal glare at me. 'And where were you *supposed* to be?'

'Wasting time in school.'

'I don't care if you think it's wasting time, you can't just go running off when you feel like it! You're supposed to be there. So we know where you are! Yourself and Stephanie disappearing in the middle of the day – that's not on, Lauren.'

I wonder whether to correct her on the fact that lunch is actually a bit later than the middle of the school day, but some shred of self-preservation shuts me up.

'What happened?' she asks. Matter-of-fact. 'What logical reason is there for you leaving school early today?'

I stare at her. 'What do you *think* happened?' I didn't get a part in the musical. I have to dress up as a boy. That's what happened. It's your school, Mum, how do you not *know* that this is what's going on? How can you not *get* it?

'I don't know, Lauren, that's why I asked.' She waits. Her lips pressed together, thin and unimpressed.

68

I turn away. 'Nothing. It was nothing. We were just bored.'

I get the That's Not Good Enough, Young Lady speech. And then this. This is the killer. 'How do you think it looks when my own daughter flaunts the rules like this?'

I think you care more about how it looks for you than how your daughter feels. But I don't say that. Of course I don't. What's the point? I shrug. It feels so clichéd. I am Sulky Moody Inexplicable Teenager. I go to my room.

Later Dad comes in to tut-tut at me, but also to let me know dinner is ready. They talk about work. I sit and eat in silence.

After dinner I vanish into music in my ears and words and images in front of me. Scroll, scroll. Some female-focused superhero movie has been announced, and there are bucketloads of comments and posts about how the world doesn't need another movie like this/how it's going to be terrible/why it's not going to include a racially diverse cast and needs to be boycotted. I start typing: *Have any of you thought about waiting until the movie's actually been made before forming a strong opinion about it?* but then hit backspace, backspace, backspace until there's nothing but blankness. I am too weary for internet fights, for being yelled at by social justice warriors as though I am even worse than the creepy men who think a female protagonist marks the end of civilisation.

I find Tara online, click on photos of her looking cute and tiny and adorable. She has red hair, a few freckles, is even wearing pigtails in a couple of these pictures.

It should have been me.

And the only one with even an inkling of how much this hurts me, how much it stings when another girl gets the thing you want, is the friend who doesn't even want to be a girl any more.

Week three, day six

I skip out early on Friday, before either Mum or Dad get home and can forbid me to go out for the evening. They've never grounded me in my life, but there's always a first time.

The bus is packed, with two guys a good bit older than me – maybe in their twenties? – eyeing me up in a way that makes me want to shudder. I hold on tight to the pole in front of me and try to look anywhere else.

Maybe they're not checking me out, maybe they're thinking I look gross and disgusting. Maybe this is arrogance on my part.

I just want to get out of there. I hop off the bus two stops early, even though the rain has turned everyone into monsters, casually jabbing everyone else with their giant umbrellas as they try to stay dry.

Justin, I remind myself as I step around puddles and friend-clusters. I get to see Justin, my lovely boyfriend, yay! The trouble is I also get to see his friends, which is less of a treat.

I wait at the entrance of the baby-hipster club where the gig is on, a place I only know by reputation. John was kicked out of here once for sneaking in vodka in a water bottle – they have a whole no-alcohol-so-we-can-be-a-safe-space-for-under-eighteens thing going on. Pity that the strong scent of weed makes it seem just a tad hypocritical.

I'm about to text Justin to see where he is, when he appears, charming smile in place, and I know that it's not the time to complain about him being late. Anyway, he's with his friends, and I'm not going to be That Girlfriend.

'Hey.'

'Hey you,' I say back, and then there's kissing, and everything around us dissolves, and suddenly the world is actually maybe an okay place to live right about now.

'Are we heading in or what?' Murphy says. Justin's friends all do that boy thing of referring to each other only by their surnames.

Justin and I come up for air. 'Right,' I say. Holding hands, we follow the others in. There's four of them, all in school with Justin, and I'm still getting to know them as individuals instead of this amorphous mass of boy-ness. In the queue, Murphy punches Cassidy in the arm and calls him a sap, for what seems like no reason. Cassidy rolls his eyes, has his own retort. Sometimes I feel like an anthropologist on a mission to uncover the secret language of teenage boys.

'Ah here, I'll pay,' Justin says when we get to the cash desk. I already have cash out. 'Nah, it's fine.'

'Come on.'

'No, really.' This is not the first time we've had this discussion. 'But I was the one who said –'

'Yeah, but if we go somewhere I want, you won't let me pay,' I counter.

'For fuck's sake,' Cassidy says, 'just shut up and let him pay.'

I spin around, but so does Justin. 'Hey, don't talk to her like that,' he says.

The pierced-nose girl at the cash desk says, bored, 'Guys, if you're not going to pay then can you get out of the queue?'

Justin pays, I pay, Cassidy and the others pay, one by one. We get our hands stamped and I try not to seem like I'm annoyed. It's just one of those days where the little things all add up. This and Cassidy being an asshole and the guys on the bus and having to be a boy in the stupid musical, and – I don't want to be here. That's what I realise in the crowd, with everyone around me talking loudly and taking selfies, all hot and sweaty and too much.

I want to be at home in my bedroom listening to a soundtrack, or curled up in bed with a book, or snuggled up with Justin, but not here.

'You want some?' Justin asks, offering me a water bottle I know contains a mix of vodka and Coke. I shake my head – not because I'm scared of getting kicked out, but because I know it's Cassidy who's responsible for sorting out alcohol. Even though I know I'm totally cutting my nose off to spite my face, because with a little bit to drink I'd be less tensed up and feeling under threat somehow.

The band comes on and everyone roars and starts snapping pictures with their phones. Justin's arms go around me, and I try not to mind that there's people to my right who keep swaying and banging into me, try not to mind when someone behind us spills a drink on my shoes. Try not to feel like an ancient granny when so much of the music sounds more like noise than anything else and I can't make out the lyrics.

(I don't want to be here.)

Justin leans in and kisses me.

I count my blessings in my head: I have a lovely boyfriend. I am out on a Friday night – actually out in town instead of at someone's house watching something on Netflix. I am trying new things and taking chances, going to gigs I wouldn't have ever gone to pre-Justin. I am stepping out of my comfort zone.

'I'm going to the bathroom,' he says in my ear after a couple of songs. A stupidly endearing thing about Justin: he says 'bathroom' rather than 'loo' or 'the jacks'.

I nod, readjust myself and try to somehow take up enough space so there'll be room for him when he comes back, that the gap he's left won't be swallowed by the people around me.

'What d'ya think?' Murphy mouths at me, nodding to the stage.

I grin, give him a thumbs-up, and then feel like an idiot. Who delivers thumbs-ups any more?

In front of me, there's some shoving going on, and then one of the guys stumbles backwards and right into me.

'Hey!' I shove him off me, or try to; he's so heavy I can't move him much.

He turns around, gives me a lazy grin. Maybe hammered. The laughter from his friends doesn't seem entirely sober. 'Hey,' he says. Steps a little closer.

Creep. 'Get *away* from me.' I hate this place I hate this place I hate this world.

More laughter from his mates. It's not funny. He slammed into me. An apology might be nice. Normal humans apologise to one another in those circumstances.

74

'Ah, there's no need for that,' he says, still with a moronic smile on his face.

And then he grabs me, so quick I can't even believe it's happening, and his stupid (yes, alcoholic) breath is too close and he's trying to kiss me and I try to wrench myself away and every limb is struggling and then we're in this tangle on the floor and there are other hands grabbing at me.

'Out you go,' a thick-necked bouncer says, pulling me up to standing.

It takes me a moment to realise he's talking to me. '*Excuse me?*'

'Can't be fighting in here. Out.'

'He grabbed me!' I say, maybe even shriek, pointing to the guy still on the floor. Cupping his bits. Looking pathetic.

'Listen, love. From where I'm standing, he's the one injured,' the bouncer says.

This is ridiculous. This can't actually be happening.

'He did start it,' Murphy chimes in. 'It wasn't her fault, he banged into her and then grabbed her . . .'

My gratitude is short-lived, because this prompts one of Mr Grabby's friends to jump in with a, 'Nah, she was being real aggressive, like.'

I can't speak. I know if I open my mouth I'll start bawling, so I walk away, only to find the bouncer following me to make sure I actually leave. He is a horrible person. I want to tell him this. But I don't want to cry in front of him.

Once outside, I go around the corner and, blurry-eyed, send Justin a text.

I will not start sobbing hysterically in the middle of the

streets like a crazy person. I will not. I will not.

Can't be fighting in here . . . she was being real aggressive, like . . .

His breath, his awful breath, and why would you even try to kiss someone you clearly had no respect for? Except that's it, maybe – it's all just some sick game, it's funny. Haha. His friends definitely think so. And he gets to stay indoors and not be the troublemaker booted out.

The rain's started up again, and my umbrella's left inside. Fuck.

Back around the corner. Another bouncer's on the door, with that same thick-neck bully look. I take a deep breath and walk past him, but he grabs me by the arm. 'Sorry, love, you can't come back in.'

I shake off his hand and glare at him. 'I've left my umbrella in here.'

He shrugs. 'That's your problem, love.'

'Stop calling me love, you – you – Neanderthal,' I say. 'You've effectively stolen my property.' And oh, yeah, I know I sound like a right bitch, I sound *exactly* like a St Agnes's girl in this moment, but this moment seems to demand it.

'Just move on, love, I'm not letting you in,' he says wearily.

'You,' I say, 'are an asshole.'

Turn on my heel, walk away, but not fast enough not to hear his little snort of laughter, like this is all so hilarious. Oh yeah? Is it really hilarious, that it's your job to be a dick to teenage girls? Really? Life goals for you, mister?

But I'm back to being weepy now, so I don't say anything, just wait around the corner.

Justin. Come on.

I look up at the guy coming around the corner, heart full of hope, but it's just a stranger. My view shoots back to my phone, but not before I see a slight smirk on the guy's face, like he thinks I like him.

I glare at his back and wish I had Medusa-like powers.

'Hey.' It's Justin. 'What happened?'

'I got kicked out,' I say, like it's not obvious, like it wasn't in my message.

'Yeah, the lads were saying, but what *happened*?'

'This creepy fucker in front of me shoves into me, and then didn't say sorry, and then grabbed me and tried to *kiss* me –' A shudder goes through my mouth as I remember; my tongue wriggles like it's trying to escape.

'And then you beat him up?' Justin sounds incredulous.

'I didn't beat him up, I tried to get him off me.'

'Yeah, but, come on, Laur, you're pretty strong.'

'I'm no— what the fuck?'

'You beat me at arm wrestling,' he reminds.

Yeah, that one time. Ugh. I'm not even sporty, just taller than average, and stupidly competitive instead of wanting to look all delicate. Which apparently makes you get treated like crap by bouncers and musical-directing teachers alike.

'So what?' I say.

'I'm just saying –' he says, and then puts up his hands. 'Come on, this is shit, but you can't go around attacking people . . .'

'I didn't *attack* anyone! He started it, and –' And then the tears. This frustration.

'Oh, baby,' Justin says, his voice gentle, as he pulls me close. It's safe here, with his arms around me, but once I calm

77

down I still need to say it. I lift my head from his shoulder, look into his eyes. 'Do you know how *not*-strong you feel when a guy grabs you?'

I mean, of course he doesn't. They beat the crap out of each other all the time in his school, but it's even-footing, or more even, and it's not . . . it's not the same. But I listen as he tells me anyway, and then he says, 'So, what do you want to do?'

'Kill someone,' I say, honestly.

'I mean the gig,' he says.

'Well, I can't go back in.'

'We could talk to them, if I talk to them maybe . . .'

'What, promise to keep an eye on me?' I roll both of mine.

'No, just . . . or we could sneak you in.'

I pause. Watch his face. 'You want to head back in.' My heart, treacherous little thing that it is, clenches.

'Well, yeah, come on. We paid in, and they're really good . . .'

No, they're not. 'You go,' I say. 'It's cool, I'll go home.'

'You sure?' He does this thing that I love, brushes his fingertips along the side of my face and pushes a bit of hair behind my ear. Part tender, part sexy.

'Yeah,' I say. Bright smile. 'Go on.'

He kisses me, and kisses me again, and then he's off, and I think: that is actually not what I meant to say. It is not cool at all.

I storm towards the bus stop, ready to take on the world. Wanting to scream. And then suddenly I'm exhausted, and I slump against the door of a now-closed gadget shop.

'Lauren?' The voice is familiar but I can't place it, until she steps closer. Felicity. 'Are you okay?'

The universe clearly wants this girl to see me at my worst at every available opportunity.

'Oh. Yeah. I'm fine.'

'You sure?' She looks genuinely concerned, as opposed to the type of 'oh, what's up?' you might get in the bathroom at school – which really means 'what's the scandal?'

'Yeah. Just heading home early.'

She nods. 'Yeeeeah,' she says slowly. 'I hear you.' She bites her lower lip. 'I was out with Amanda and Shelley and all that gang.'

I try not to look too stunned. That's the crowd she's been hanging out with since she started at our school. 'Not fun?'

'Nope.'

The bus arrives and we get on, sitting next to each other. Silence for a bit, but not the terribly awkward kind. And then I say, 'Congrats on the musical.' I am surprised to find I even mean it.

'Thanks. I'm really excited.' Her face lights up, and then she calms herself down, like she's remembered it's not cool to care about such things.

'It's cool. Break a leg. Break two.'

'I thought you were really good, by the way.'

'Huh?'

'The singing. And the dancing. And – I thought you should've got a part.'

Something inside me lightens. 'Oh, well,' I still say. Like it doesn't matter.

'Seriously,' she adds.

I am quiet for a moment and then I say, 'Thanks, Felicity.'

She winces. 'Call me Fee. Please. I hate that name.'

'Really? It's so –'

'It's so Enid Blyton!'

'That's the whole point!' I say, a little more animated than I mean to be. 'Like, she's got one in the *St Clare's* series, who's a musical genius, and then another one in *Malory Towers* – she's Darrell's sister, and Darrell is an absolute *legend*.'

Felicity – Fee – makes a face. 'Yeah. I just never got into the school stories.'

Just when I was starting to like her.

'*The Faraway Tree*, now . . .' she continues.

Be still my heart! I nearly want to make her a friendship bracelet.

Just before we get off the bus, a tiny memory crawls into my brain. 'Hey. Do you really think God is an elephant?'

She gives me a puzzled look.

'The retreat,' I remind her.

Fee bursts out laughing. 'Oh yeah!' She shrugs. 'Elephants are the only thing I can draw.'

Week three, day seven

'Where're you off to?' Mum asks.

I pause in the hallway, my coat only half on. 'Town. There's a Q Club meeting on.'

I can see the dilemma play out across her face: will she tell me I can't go because of skipping out of school early on Thursday? Or would it be a bad message to send, telling her not-straight daughter that she can't go to her support group?

(A slight pang: the whole coming-out-to-Mum thing only happened because I was ranting about Mrs O'Connor's religion class about a year ago and said I might end up marrying a woman so there, and Mum looked at me and went 'really?' and I said 'yeah' and she said 'okay' and that was it. Complaining about my teachers – and then complaining about the teachers she worked with – used to be *how we talked*.)

'Go on, then, but I want you home early.'

'Sure,' I say.

She leans in for a quick hug.

'Will we watch a movie or something later?' I ask suddenly.

'Oh, pet, I don't know if I've time, I've a lot of work to do.'

'Okay,' I say. Bright smile.

I want to tell her about what happened last night, the creepy guy, Justin not getting it, but I realise I can't trust her to be on my side. I know it's not that she doesn't love me or anything like that, I'm not a moron. It's just like she doesn't have the *time*.

This is a proper facilitated session at the Q Club headquarters, so we go around the group and talk about our Feelings and it all feels a little bit AA.

'On the one hand,' Marc says, rasping a little to lower his voice, 'it's like I'm becoming who I'm supposed to be, and on the other hand it's like there are still people who are never going to accept that.'

Steph is nodding and doing supportive-face. I can't watch it. I stare at the floor instead, scratchy blue carpet that reminds me of school.

A nudge in my side from Ellie. I look up. My turn to say anything if I want. 'I'm fine,' I say, with a shrug.

Ellie snorts. I nudge her right back.

And then it's her turn. 'Yeah, nothing too traumatic recently. School's really stressful, but . . .' She shrugs. 'What can you do?'

'It's really hard being out in school,' Marc says solemnly.

'I think she meant, like, homework, exams, that kind of thing,' I say with just the teensiest bit of an edge.

'Don't be a bitch,' Ellie murmurs in my ear. Nicely, though. To the group she says, 'Yeah, well, everything, really.'

Why is it that when people try to be fair and nice to everyone they end up betraying someone? I stay quiet as the session progresses. Maybe I shouldn't even be here. I have a boyfriend, even if I'm still a bit annoyed with him about last night. I am a cis girl even if I want to rip out all my reproductive organs and sell them to the highest bidder or hide my body in the most shapeless clothes I can find so that if creepy men look at me or grab me at least it won't be my fault. You only get sympathy here if you are defining yourself as something else.

The anger boils and boils until I am almost shaking with it. 'Excuse me,' I mutter, and stand up, make my way out the door, feeling almost light-headed.

Then out through the main door and into the street, where the air is cold on my face and I try to breathe normally but it comes in gasps.

Suddenly the door opens again and Ellie assesses the situation. One hand on my back, rubbing circles. 'Breathe in . . . out . . . in . . . out . . .'

That horrible panicky feeling subsides. 'Thanks,' I say, sheepishly.

She shrugs. 'What's up?'

I gesture towards the door. 'I don't – I can't – I'm so sick of everything being about –'

'Marc,' she supplies.

'Yeah.' I sag against the wall. 'But we can't say that, 'cause then it's being transphobic, but like . . . everything. Everything gets brought back to that.'

'It's a stage a lot of people go through. Right now transitioning is the most important thing in his life and this is probably the only space he has to talk about it.'

'Yeah, well, he talks to Steph all the fucking time about it too.'

'Ahhhh,' Ellie says knowingly.

'What?'

'Jealous,' she sing-songs.

'No, I just think that Marc is –' I pause. I don't want to say 'a bad influence'. How prim and proper.

'Laur,' Ellie says seriously, 'I think you're on the verge of saying something really shitty, so don't, okay?'

Something snaps in me. 'Yes, heaven forbid anyone *dare* question the idea of suddenly wanting to change your gender because your new best friend is trans. Sure, let's go in and chop off Steph's tits right now, why don't we?'

Ellie gives me this *look*. Like that was exactly the sort of thing she expected. It is too self-righteous for words. I glare at her.

'Be like that,' she says coldly, and slams the door behind her.

Before

I am there the first time you kiss a girl. It's the same night I have my first kiss ever. You've been kissed by a boy before, once, awkwardly, not-quite-consensually, when you were eleven. You told me this and mimed the sloppy-tongue action so graphically that even though I mostly find your tongue alluring it was totally disgusting.

It's a Q Club thing. Obviously. Our world has expanded: we are no longer two loners in the wilderness of St Agnes's but girls who have found their people. There are the regulars, and then there are friends-of-friends, and the lines between online and 'real' dissolve much more than they ever have before. Because online-me is not online-friends with anyone else from school, or anyone in my family (people who let their parents get on Facebook are just weird, never mind adding them as friends), and yet she is more me than school-me, exchanging thoughts and gifs with people from all over the world.

And now we're both getting to know people online who we then see in person a couple of weeks later. And tonight is a party – okay, 'party' might be too grand a word for hanging out under the trees in a park drinking vodka out of Coke bottles. But everything's fizzing and I know something will happen. It's been building for weeks.

I talk to John for a while, and I decide I am going to make things happen for him. He's been eyeing up this guy Rich for ages and I think there's definitely something there, so I finally say, 'John, you need to score Rich.'

John looks at me like I've suggested he kick a kitten. 'What? No . . .'

'Yes. You want to, I bet he's up for it – what's the worst that can happen?'

'Death,' John says gloomily.

'Okay, how about this? I'll ask him, see what he says, worst-case scenario you avoid him for the rest of the evening.'

'No . . .' John says again, hiding his head in his hands.

'Come on. Pleeeeeeeeeeeeease?' I do puppy-dog eyes at him.

I don't know why exactly it's so important to me right now. There's just something pushing at me to make the kissing start.

'Okay,' John says in a tiny voice.

I leap up, march over to where Rich is talking to a couple of the girls, and draw him away by crooking my finger. 'John. What d'you think?'

Rich immediately knows where to look, which confirms my suspicions that he's been eyeing him up.

'Don't look!' I hiss.

But it's too late: their eyes meet. Panic flashes across John's face and punches me in the heart: please let me not have made this worse. Please let it not be hideously awkward.

And then before I know it they're properly kissing, really

going at it, and a few people cheer and then get on with life, and that thing that I wanted to happen has happened. The line has been crossed from friends-hanging-out to people kissing.

That's the moment I see you, your hair still long then, with your lips on someone else's. I don't recognise her, but she has prettier hair than mine, and I bet it's silky-smooth. Your hand is on her cheek.

That's the thing that I notice. Not the fact that you're swapping saliva, that your faces are smushed together, but that you're doing this tiny tender thing that makes something inside me jump.

'Stop gawking,' says someone who I think is a beautiful boy but will later learn is Ellie.

I swallow more vodka. Ellie hugs me even though we have never met before, then goes and chats with her friends. I look at my phone for a while and watch as the sky darkens. Eventually a couple of guys in uniforms – in my tipsy state I can't tell if they're proper cops or just some kind of park security types – approach us and we know we have to go, so we're all gathering up our stuff and racing towards the exit.

There's the 'where do we go now?' question, and it seems like no one's parents are conveniently away or neglectful or indulgent, so we end up wandering off in different directions.

There's no point in saying goodbye to anyone. I slink off, but then. There you are, racing after me. 'Hey, wait up!'

I stop and turn. 'Hey.'

'You abandoner!' you say dramatically.

'You were busy!'

You laugh. 'I'm a woman of the world.'

My mouth drops open. 'You didn't – was there – did you do stuff?'

'You have a filthy mind, Lauren Carroll. We just kissed.'

'Well, good. I mean, in a park, like.'

'Yeah, the first time I get eaten out I'd prefer to be inside.'

'And I'm the one with the filthy mind?' I say incredulously. I try not to picture that scenario, but there are interesting sensations happening somewhere between my legs.

You skip and twirl and it's like you're a kid, albeit a kid who thinks about sex a lot. 'I kissed a girl,' you sing to a tune of your own, thankfully avoiding doing a Katy Perry impression.

'Go you,' I say, trying to sound enthusiastic.

Maybe girl-kissing has given you psychic powers or maybe vodka-drinking has made me transparent but you stop and say, 'Oh my God, you're jealous.'

'I am not.' I pause, and opt for a version of the truth. 'It's just weird watching people pair up.'

'Jealous!' you sing.

'Fuck off,' I say, more grumpily than I intend.

We both stop. We're on the corner of a main road, just about to turn left for a shortcut home. The sky's dark but the road is still well lit, lampposts everywhere. We are both in a very public space, cars zipping past, and not, because there aren't that many people actually walking on the road and it feels like those in the cars can't see us, can't touch us.

You hug me. And then it's just the tiniest kiss, not even with terrifying swirly-tongue action: just your lips pressed against mine, so sweetly and gently. Like a fairy tale. This is the kind of pure kiss that wakes up a princess.

'I think I'm turning into a slut,' you say after a second of silence, and we both crack up.

'Come on, let's get home.'

Week four, day one

At three in the morning I am staring at my phone. There are messages. There is noise. Just none of it directly for me. Updates on people's individual profiles, new messages in group chats. Nothing from Justin, who doesn't see anything wrong with choosing his friends and crap music over his girlfriend. Nothing from Ellie, not that I was really expecting it. Nothing from Steph, no wondering 'hey what's up with walking out of Q Club?'

I am not worth caring about. Thanks for making that clear, everyone.

I find Fee's profile, add her, and then go through all my old updates and make most of them private. I am a blank slate. I am starting over.

Mum has time for me today, apparently. 'Do you want to watch something this afternoon?' she asks. 'Dad's going into the office – we could get a takeaway?'

I don't bother asking why Dad's doing a Sunday in the office at this time of year; it's always a busy time. 'Chinese?' I say.

'Sure.'

She lets me choose, so I find my *Rent* DVD and stick it on. Usually I love it. But today all the characters annoy me. I want to slap Idina Menzel. And I *adore* her.

The doorbell rings, and I hit pause while Mum goes to answer it and pay for the food. I join her in the kitchen, messing around with napkins and cutlery and transferring things from paper and foil containers into proper dishes.

'Can I've a glass?' I ask as she unscrews the cork from a bottle of white wine. Chancing my arm a bit.

'A *small* glass,' she says.

I try not to look too pleased.

Apart from one glass of champagne last New Year's Eve I have never consumed alcohol in a parent's presence before. It is for friends, nights out, silliness. But there's something soothing about sitting here at home, on the couch with Mum, with a glass of wine to sip at. I suddenly understand women in sitcoms who open a bottle after a stressful day. It's not a getting-hammered thing, not like a proper party. It's just the liquid equivalent of having your hair stroked. Calming.

'I wish we were doing *Rent* in school,' I say wistfully.

'Not sure the staff would have gone for that,' Mum says, laughing.

'What do you think of the one we *are* doing?'

She shrugs. 'I don't know enough about it. It's up to Elaine – eh, Ms Lynch, and Mrs O'Connor, anyway.'

'I know their first names, Mum, it's not a big secret.'

She sighs. 'I know.'

91

On the screen, Idina Menzel delivers her great line about women in rubber.

'I can't *imagine* why you think anyone at school would have a problem with this,' I say, and Mum laughs.

Week four, day two

We all call it 'community service' even though the actual term is 'community outreach' – weeks where school finishes early and we spend our afternoons doing virtuous things like helping out at charity shops or packing bags in the local supermarket and then carrying them to people's cars (that one sounds a bit more like child labour, really) or picking up rubbish in the local parks.

This is one of those weeks, and I am on park duty. Here is an example of the ridiculousness of my school: we can't wear our school uniforms for this but we do have to wear our school tracksuits. One of the PE teachers walks a group of us to the park down the road and hands out gloves and black sacks.

'Oh, the glamour,' I mutter to no one in particular.

'I've been waiting my whole life for this,' someone to the left of me says.

I look over. Tiny, perfect Tara, stealer of ideal musical roles, is grinning at me. I smile back before I remember to hate her.

'This is so totally gross,' someone else says, in what sounds like a perfect parody of a Valley Girl accent but is in fact her real voice. Amanda, cool girl and former friend to Fee, has

93

contorted her face into sheer horror at the prospect of picking up crisp packets.

'I can't believe this is legal,' someone else chimes in.

We get a pep talk from our teacher before venturing off on our exciting adventure. There are strict instructions not to go near anything that looks dangerous, like abandoned needles or broken glass. By the end of the afternoon some drug paraphernalia would be a welcome change from cigarette butts and chocolate bar wrappers, but alas. This park is just not dodgy enough for such things.

But it is a distraction from other stuff. Like musicals and uncommunicative boyfriends and, well, other people.

Week four, day four

By Wednesday I am starting to feel almost okay. Almost happy. Plans with Justin for Friday night – house party at Cassidy's, which I'm hoping we can either escape from early or else will have lots of booze. Fee has accepted my friend request and I ran into her and Tara in the corridors yesterday at lunch time and we walked down to the shops together to get chocolate, which was weirdly nice and normal. Friendship, casual friendship, like it should be, not like Ellie making everything *political*.

And then last night Steph sent me a link to a blog about musicals, with a smiley face at the end of the message.

Maybe this is what normal feels like.

But then the doorbell rings on Wednesday night and I hear the voices and go peer out the window to check the car and yes. It's Geraldine. Steph's mum.

She's in floods of tears and Mum is taking her into her study to pour her a glass of wine and talk soothingly at her. From upstairs I can only hear the sounds, but I know the story. This is not the first time this has happened.

I tiptoe out of my room, creep down the stairs. Dad is in

his own office, upstairs – a sliver of light escaping from under the door – so there's no one to stop me from being nosy and hovering outside the study. Which is a terrible trait and one that classic school stories would disapprove of – eavesdroppers can only expect to hear bad things about themselves if they listen at doors – but I want to know. Need to know. When there are crying people in your house you want to find out what's going on, even to reassure yourself that everything's okay.

'She just keeps saying she's in the wrong body . . .' That's Geraldine. 'The wrong body, I mean, I don't even know what that means. She's looking up all this stuff online about hormones and she's . . .' Sobbing.

I try to imagine if Mum is hugging her, but I think maybe not a full-on hug. A pat on the shoulder, a squeeze of the arm.

'She's fifteen, I can't let her . . . She wants to go to the doctor and talk about it!'

Vague comforting noises, then Mum: 'Well, it might be worth taking her to the doctor. Just for a chat.'

'I don't want her to think I'm taking this nonsense seriously,' Geraldine says, suddenly sharp. 'She needs to snap out of it.'

Ugh, see, that's the thing. When Geraldine says it, it sounds awful. Patronising and judgemental and narrow-minded. Like no one could ever realise they need to live as another gender, or feel their body is wrong for them.

I've never liked Geraldine. The first time I went back to Steph's house, only a few weeks into secondary school, she opened the conversation with, 'Stephanie, for God's sake, brush your hair.' She's the kind of woman who thinks not using a coaster under your glass is the worst possible thing you could ever do. Well, that or have a gender identity crisis, I suppose.

'Well, Geraldine, if you say it like that she'll get defensive,' Mum says in her sensible voice. I hear pouring happening, definitely into glasses and not mugs. I would put good money on Dad having to drive Geraldine home later tonight.

When in doubt, ask the internet. The lights in the house are all out now – I was right about Dad giving Geraldine a lift home – except for my bedside lamp.

Scrolling, scrolling, through pop culture news and pictures of cats and weird science facts and friends' rants and there it is. Steph's profile is no longer Steph. Steph is now Evan, which sounds firstly super-American and secondly super-influenced-by-Marc.

Just to let you know that using my birth name or misgendering me is really fucking transphobic btw, so you can go to hell.

I look at the words and I want to know who exactly is going to be looking at this that would even do that. It's not like Geraldine does social media. It's not like Steph – Evan, Evan – is friends with all the girls at school. The people who can read this are Q Club people or other friends St— *Evan* has made online, people who think that 'cis' or 'hetero' or 'white' are insults. (Which. You know. I get it but sometimes I just want to punch them. More so recently.)

Misgendering. I look at the little box for gender which has been hidden from Steph's profile since the summer and is now proudly 'male'. Well. There we have it. It's official. Decided. End of discussion.

***

97

Staring at the computer makes me sympathetic to Geraldine in a way that makes me uncomfortable. She's so easy to upset anyway. So very – not quite hysterical (problematic word!), exactly, but hypersensitive to anything not-quite-normal.

(And isn't 'normal' problematic too, I say to myself.)

I skim the comments, spying Marc early on, full of pride and hearts, and the rest are fairly similar. Then someone's said 'no need to be so aggressive omg we get it!' With a smiley-face. And Evan's response is to link to an article about 'tone policing', nothing else.

I start typing a reply to that and then stop. I start and stop. Words turn into sentences turn into paragraphs and then I delete them all.

Who the fuck even *are* you, Evan?

Before

When we get into third year everything's different. The summer of hanging out with people who get it – who do things like write poems about being gay or feeling like they're in the wrong body and about how much it sucks when the world is shitty about it – has given us an extra aura of confidence.

It's one of those things that's only possible to see after returning to a familiar place. In books there's always this line about how when people return to their childhood homes they look smaller. School doesn't look smaller but it feels it. It is a tinier part of the world. We've always known this in theory but now we really know.

Our eye-rolls in class become more pronounced. Not all of our subjects – not when Ms Lynch is explaining something in English, because we both love her (me more than you, I think), or when we're trying to wrap our brains around maths (because I'm in the idiots' class, you in the genius one). But when Mrs O'Connor goes on with her nonsense, or Mr Byrne in history says something unbelievably problematic – then we're on it. Hands in the air, sometimes. We ask Mr Byrne what the women were doing in whatever country and time period we're talking about and every single time he looks like he wants to strangle us.

It doesn't matter that the cool girls think we're weird. It doesn't matter that we don't bargain our way into nightclubs in loud giggly groups, tottering on high heels. It doesn't matter we don't turn up for school wearing three inches of make-up – and isn't it weird that we're the ones who are actually into girls and not bothering with this? Who are they trying to impress?

None of this matters because you're my best friend and even though we are not together-together (though I bet if you asked anyone in school they'd presume we are) there is occasional kissing, just silly, no big deal, and we are kissing other people too, but. But. Whatever it is that goes beyond just-friendship? It makes me feel stronger and braver and happier than I ever have before.

Week four, day six

School won't call me by my new name because my mum hasn't given her permission. Why the fuck does it matter if she gives permission or not? It's not her life. Principal says I can ask teachers individually but she can't change my name on the roll call, which basically means that they're not going to take it seriously and are going to keep using a name that is NOT ME – which is clearly what she WANTS, the transphobic bitch.

I stare at the update on my phone. Evan's latest shared moment with the world, or at least the enclosed world of his profile, involves being an absolute – well, there's a four-letter word that comes to mind but that'd probably be transphobic now too. I mentally replace it with *dick*. There we go. There has to be something clever and amusing to be said about how wanting a dick makes you act like one, but all I can do is think about the time Steph slept over at my house a few days after her grandfather died and I woke up and padded downstairs to see – through a slightly ajar door – her and Mum in the kitchen, talking seriously over mugs of something, probably herbal tea or hot chocolate. I watched and listened for a moment and then I went back up to bed, not feeling jealous or anything – just weirdly glad that Steph was able to talk to my mother about grief and loss in a way that I knew she wasn't able to with Geraldine.

Don't read the comments, I remind myself, but like anyone is actually ever able to listen to that advice. More names I don't know – online trans friends, I am guessing – jumping in to say how bullshit this all is.

IT'S AN ALL-GIRLS SCHOOL, I want to scream at them. And also, MY MOTHER IS NOT A BITCH.

A text message alert comes in, and I expect it to be Evan apologising, or maybe Ellie or John saying 'what the actual fuck', but it's Justin. Shit. I need to get ready.

Cassidy had better have something very alcoholic waiting for us at his house.

'Girls are hanging out over there,' Cassidy tells me when we arrive.

'Why are you segregating us?' I ask, bemused.

'What the fuck?' He squints at me.

'Why are – oh, never mind. What are we playing?' He is an idiot. I must remember this. He may be Justin's friend but he is a moron. I will play games with my lovely boyfriend and Murphy, who's waving us over, and not go join the girls sitting on the other couch taking selfies.

We make it through the first couple of rounds of this new fantasy game before getting antsy for food and drink, and it's only when we get up to go to the kitchen I see just who the girls are. I know a couple of them vaguely but we've never exactly had deep meaningful conversations, but they're all the same type – blandly pretty. Lots of make-up, clothes that girls wear in magazines, perfect duck-face pouting for the camera. And among the four that are here tonight is Sandra from Q Club.

My eyes catch hers and she stares for a second, until she recognises me. We're out of context here. But then she does – I can see it – and she looks away. Pretends she hasn't seen me, doesn't know me, whatever.

There actually is some kind of official policy about not outing people in Q Club to others, a 'what happens in Vegas stays in Vegas' deal, but this feels closer to 'eh, I don't, like, *know* you?'

I wonder if she's here with a boyfriend and is just pretending to be queer to be cool. Which, yeah, is not something you're supposed to think about other people but sometimes it is a thing that happens.

(Says the girl here with *her* boyfriend. I know. I just get a bad vibe from Sandra.)

'You're such a faggot,' Cassidy is saying to someone in the kitchen when we get there, some guy whose arm is being punched. Boys. Honestly.

'Yay homophobia!' I say cheerfully, and suddenly everyone's looking at me. Cassidy, Murphy, the arm-punchee, a couple of other guys, Justin.

'It's grand, no one here is gay,' Murphy says.

'Yeah, well, they wouldn't want to admit to it around this guy, would they?'

Cassidy laughs. 'Maguire, for fuck's sake, keep your woman under control.'

I stare at Justin, who looks embarrassed. Mortified.

And then I realise it's not Cassidy who's making that happen. It's me.

Justin genuinely wishes I would just shut up. At least around his friends. Don't be a crazy girl, Lauren. One of *those* girls.

'You,' I say to Cassidy, in my best private-school-bitch voice ever, 'must have the tiniest dick known to mankind.'

Whistles and laughs from the rest of them, but they're already behind me. I storm into the living room, get my jacket and bag.

I do not have to like my boyfriend's friends. And I do not.

And now the big question: in my great dramatic flounce-away, will that boyfriend follow me or not?

I close the front door behind me, and walk down the driveway. It's colder now, night-time cold, and even though it's a seemingly safe little cul-de-sac I still don't want to hang around here indefinitely.

I count to one hundred. Slowly, the way I used to in Mass every Sunday before my parents stopped making me go. Still no sign of Justin, and nothing on my phone either.

I want him to come out here. But only if he's on my side. Ready to admit I was right to point out the grossness of Cassidy saying that, instead of being embarrassed about his girlfriend Making a Scene.

Two hundred. Three hundred.

At five hundred, I put my hands in my jacket pockets and begin the walk home.

There are only bad things on the internet. Somewhere in America another unarmed black man's been shot by thuggish white cops. Somewhere in rural Ireland a man has murdered his wife. Sorry, *allegedly* murdered his wife, as the anonymous men commenting on articles are insisting, alongside their suggestion she might have been a 'dirty slag' having it off with someone else.

Suicide bombings. Female genital mutilation. Poverty and injustice. I click and click and this world, this fucking world, is too hard and too much. I don't know how to live in it.

. . . *keep your woman under control* . . .

I take out my phone, ready to ask Justin if he really, genuinely doesn't *see* it, the links between saying something like that at a party to those vile internet comments to being the guy who kills his wife. But I know the answer already, don't I?

At two in the morning when I still can't sleep, and Mum and Dad are safely snoring – I can hear them both, even though Mum swears she never snores and Dad refuses to believe he can possibly be as loud as Mum says – I creep downstairs.

The 'liquor cabinet' (does anyone call it that any more?) is full of things that invite Q Club gathering flashbacks. Vodka (shots of doom, high chance of instant vomit) and gin (crying on the stairs about how terrible the world is) and whiskey (just say no, kids). But in the next cupboard there are normal drinks: bottles of craft beer (Dad's, or Mum's if she's having a curry), bottles of wine (Mum's, or for guests). I pick one of each, ones that there are duplicates of. A screw-cap white wine and some fancy IPA that I open with a fridge-magnet bottle-opener before going back up to my room.

I want this blanket around me. I want to be safe. I want to sleep.

Week five, day one

No word from Justin. No word at all. The weekend is creeping to a close and even though he's updated stuff online – including photos of himself and 'the lads' at Cassidy's on Friday night – he hasn't bothered getting in touch.

So. Fine. *Fine.*

(I know, I know, I'll probably realise this is just stupid hormones again and be super-apologetic and grovelling. But this feels different. Firmer.)

'Everything okay?' Mum asks me after dinner, while Dad is loading up the dishwasher.

She knows, I realise. Even though she doesn't know about Justin (at least officially – but mothers always suspect, don't they?), she knows something's up. Senses it.

I shrug. 'Yeah, fine.'

I wait to be nudged further and instead I hear, 'Have you been talking much to Stephanie lately?'

Oh. 'Eh, a bit.'

'Geraldine's very upset about it all. It must be so hard on her.'

I say nothing. Stare at the table.

'And I can't do anything in school unless she's on board; we have to respect the parents' wishes . . .'

My head jerks up. 'Stop it.'

'What?'

'Stop it. You're the one who made this whole big deal about boundaries. If I don't get to talk to you about school stuff, you don't get to talk to me about it.' My voice is shaking. This is maybe the first time I have said something so directly, so out-loud, to her.

Mum opens and closes her mouth like a goldfish and then says tightly, 'Fine. You're right. I won't say anything to you.'

I hate it when she does that voice. I am always in the wrong, with that voice, and she is always right. I feel about eight years old instead of sixteen.

'Okay,' I say in just as cold a voice, and I go upstairs to my room.

Steph is now Evan and calls you a bitch, Mother Dearest. But do by all means focus on one of your students instead of your own daughter. Go for it. Go right ahead.

107

Week five, day four

What's the only thing more cringe-inducing than a bunch of simpering girls playing a bunch of simpering girls in a musical? Half of those girls actually having to play the boys who jump in towards the end of the song and sing about how these girls literally can't live without them.

The song in question is called 'The Boy Friend' (title drop alert) which is all about, well, wanting a boyfriend. Because that's what every young lady wants, you see. The song is not subtle. Or empowering. Or anything.

'Put more feeling into it!' Mrs O'Connor urges us, but the only feeling I have for this song is disdain.

She has arranged us so that the 'boys' are facing the girls, which means I'm right across from a sulky St— *Evan*. Face like thunder, even as we go again for one more rendition of the song.

I try to put on a deep voice for the boy parts, but I don't want to screw up my throat for this thing. I'm not saying my great dream is to rack up a whole load of starring roles on Broadway or anything, but how depressing would it be to wreck your voice for the sake of the chorus in a school musical?

If you were one of the leads, now, that might be different . . .

but they're not even here. They get special rehearsal sessions. Not like us plebs.

'Stephanie!' Mrs O'Connor explodes suddenly, just as we're coming to the last line. 'Get that *scowl* off your face!'

Evan mutters something I can't quite hear.

'What was that?'

'I *said*, I don't want to be here.'

'Well, young lady, sometimes we all have to do things –'

I can sense it before it happens; Evan storms off.

How's she supposed to know, Evan, come on, I think. She doesn't realise what she's said.

But then I think about how much you really want someone to come and look after you when you've been so upset that you storm off.

I follow, ignoring the 'and where are *you* going?' demand at my back.

'Hey!' I call.

Evan turns around. 'Hey.'

'She's – just ignore her.'

'She got a letter.' This said in a tiny voice. Tiny but angry.

'What?'

'Mrs O'Connor. I . . . just want them to use a name that's *me*. So I left a note for all my teachers. And. Yeah.'

'But, like, if your mum's saying it's not okay, they have to –'

'Oh, Jesus, Lauren, do you fucking *get* it at all?' Tiny angry is now loud angry. In-my-face angry.

'Don't *yell* at me.'

'You're just like your mother,' Evan spits.

There is fire beneath my skin. 'You are such an asshole. Do

109

you even *see* it? You've suddenly decided you want to be a boy and you've turned into the worst kind. You're a creepy fucking misogynist.'

'How dare –'

'Because let's face it,' I say, hissing now, 'you just don't want to be a girl. You think girl-bodies are gross. You've made that obvious. So I'm really sorry you hate yourself, but don't take it out on me.'

Evan is saying more, but I can't hear it. I'm screaming and shouting and covering my ears and then he's shouting and then there's a hand on my arm and a voice in my ear.

'What's going on, guys?' Ms Lynch says.

'Nothing,' we say in unison.

'Yeah, sure, two friends yelling at each other in the corridor – sounds like nothing to me.'

'We're not friends,' I snap, shaking her hand off and walking away.

But not before I hear Ms Lynch say gently, 'Evan, do you want to come for a walk, we'll have a chat?'

Hot tears fill up my eyes and I hate that it looks like I'm sad when I am so, so angry.

Week five, day five

Crying in school again today at lunch time, hiding in the bathroom. It must be stupid lady-hormones, but even the thought of that just makes it so much worse. Crazy girl. Unloved. Unwanted. Rightly so.

The door opens, and I press a clump of toilet paper to my mouth to muffle the stupid sobs.

'You do it,' someone whispers.

'No, you.'

'You.'

First-years daring each other to light a cigarette? I roll my eyes, and then decide to be a good human being. And also I don't want the hassle of a school evacuation.

'Don't smoke in here, there're smoke detectors,' I call out wearily. I am a wise old crone imparting hard-won knowledge.

'Lauren?' a voice says.

I mop up my face, open the stall door. Fee and Tara are hovering there like anxious mothers.

'Are you okay?' Fee asks.

'You looked sad earlier,' Tara adds, and I am sort of weirdly flattered that she noticed. We have International Cuisine (basically Home Ec dressed up for Transition Year to make it seem more exciting) together, but it's a big class and I feel like power-wise the noticing that should happen is from me to her, not the other way around. She's playing Maisie. She's more important than me.

'I'm fine,' I say, automatically.

They look at each other, and I can see an eyes-only version of the earlier conversation happening.

'We're going to McDonald's after school if you want to come,' Tara says finally.

I look at them. Normal girls. Ordinary girls. Maybe this is exactly who I need. It's not like anyone else cares.

'Yeah, okay,' I say. 'Sure.'

'So tell me something,' Fee says as I'm in the middle of sprinkling an extra packet of salt over my chips. 'What's the story with you and Mrs O'Connor?'

'What d'you mean?' I shrug. 'She just doesn't like me.'

'Yeah, but she *really* doesn't like you. I mean, like I said to you, you so should've got one of the main parts.'

Tara nods at this, which surprises me. 'You were *so* good,' she agrees, a hand up to cover the fact that she's speaking through a mouthful of chicken. 'But,' she adds, turning to Fee, 'Lauren's too much of a rebel. Mrs O'Connor would never pick her.'

'I am *not* a rebel,' I say, and to be fair, Fee seems surprised by this assessment of me too.

'Ah you are, you're always getting into these arguments with her in religion class. Like about gay marriage or whatever. You practically had a screaming match with her that time she

112

started going on about the eighth amendment.'

My face heats up. Not because it's not true, but because I didn't realise until now that there was anyone other than Steph – Evan – noticing this. Noticing me. And thinking about it in a way that wasn't just rolling their eyes over bothering to care about anything that takes place in a classroom.

'What's the eighth amendment?' Fee asks.

This is the point where I remember that she is one of the normal girls.

'Felicity Nugent, I am shocked.' Tara shakes her head in mock outrage.

'And appalled,' I join in.

Fee sticks her tongue out. 'Go on, smarty-pantses, educate me.'

While I am wondering whether that is in fact the correct plural of smartypants, Tara says, 'It's the whole thing about how you can't get an abortion here.'

'Ah yeah,' she says. 'Unless it's like . . .'

'No unless,' I say. 'Like, you could be thirteen and abused by your dad and get knocked up and still no abortion for you.'

Fee looks at me, horrified. 'Oh my God, Lauren, did that happen to you?'

Tara starts snorting with laughter. I've never heard – or noticed – her laughing before. It sounds ridiculous and undignified and also very endearing.

'It was a hypothetical!' I reassure her.

Tara's still cracking up.

'Stop it, you bitch,' Fee says, jabbing her in the arm. 'How was I supposed to know?'

113

She's mostly joking but I see a tiny flicker of uncertainty in her eyes, something I recognise.

'Yeah, exactly,' I say. 'I could be seriously psychologically scarred and Tara'd just be there laughing at me.'

We both look terribly smug until Tara says, 'Yeah, but given that you use that example *every single time* you and Mrs O'Connor get into this argument . . .'

Fee laughs now, a pealing thing like bells. Something tugs at me, low down in my belly, and I have a terrible feeling it's the beginnings of a crush. Not what I need in school. Too torturous. No crushes on straight girls, Lauren. 'We should get Imelda knocked up, see what she says then.'

'Ugh, no one would go near her,' I say.

'She's not bad looking,' Tara notes. 'Pity about her personality.'

'She prays at the start of every rehearsal,' Fee informs me.

So this is what your jaw dropping feels like. 'Seriously?'

They both nod, exchanging eye-rolls, and I am too caught up in the absurdity of this to be jealous of their exclusive inner-circle main-cast-only rehearsals.

'I feel like she's going to get to college and go mad,' Tara says. 'Like, go totally Satanic. My brother's a Satanist, you know.'

'He is not,' Fee says.

'He is, seriously. Like, a crap one, I think, but he's got the actual Satanic bible and he's all goth and everything.'

'How old is he?' I ask.

'Fourteen.'

'Oh, come on!' Fee shakes her head. 'That's such a phase.'

'Yeah, probably,' Tara says.

I think of Evan. Of Geraldine.

But then I also think about how I could so easily kiss either of these girls right now.

Maybe I am secretly a Lesbian Predator in denial. Except I have read ten bajillion online articles about consent so I'd never actually do anything unless it was all okay and mutual. Like, we could be stroking each other's hair at a sleepover and then –

Focus, Lauren.

'So how's your boyfriend?' Fee asks, and for a second I mishear and think she means the musical.

'Oh. Ugh.'

'Ugh?' Fee says.

'You have a *boyfriend*?' Tara says at the same time, and then blushes.

'She definitely has a boyfriend and does not find me attractive,' Fee says firmly.

'Oh God,' I groan, burying my face in my hands.

'But what about you and Steph?' Tara wants to know.

'Don't ask,' I mutter.

'Waaaait, what's this about her and Steph?' Fee squeals, turning to Tara.

'Nothing,' I say. 'There's nothing. And I no longer have a boyfriend either, even though he hasn't actually bothered breaking up with me.'

Cue an hour of discussing and dissecting the situation and Boys in General and already I'm bored. *They just don't say what they feel . . . I don't think they even notice . . . They just want . . . They don't care . . .*

But then I think about that night at the gig with the plethora of assholes, and I wonder if maybe all that men-are-from-

Mars-women-are-from-Venus bullshit has more truth in it than not. If it's just that simple, that binary.

(Fuck binaries, though, am I right?)

(Am I?)

(Why do I have to overthink everything?)

There's too much swirling around in my brain, made worse when the girls invite me to come along shopping with them – the shopping centre nearest us stays open till nine on Fridays. I text Mum to let her know I've had dinner, will be home later.

Unlike with Evan, there are no charity or vintage shops in sight – instead it's mass-market chains like Penneys and H&M, where there are girls-girls-girls everywhere. I look despairingly at tiny T-shirts with 'bitch' and 'slut' and 'porn star' emblazoned on the front. Don't get me started about anything with words on the ass. No one needs to read anyone else's ass. Ever.

It's not all like this, obviously, but it just feels so cheap and tacky. Low-cost imitations of fancy brands, items of clothing that are probably made in sweatshops by seven-year-old kids.

'I'm going to take off,' I say to Fee and Tara after the fifth or so shop. I'm empty-handed. Fee is carrying around one of those onesie-type things in a paper bag. Tara tries on everything and then decides not to buy anything, even though she's tiny and dainty and precisely the right size for these kinds of shops.

Fee checks her phone for the time. 'I need to get home, actually. Will we head to the bus stop?'

And so we do, weaving through the crowds of Christmas shoppers laden down with bags. The lights and decorations hanging from the high ceiling of the shopping centre feel cheap and tacky, and even when we get outside, the twinkling lights against the darkness don't seem as magical as they should. It doesn't feel like Christmas is almost here. Not the way it used to when I was little. I can't get excited about it.

'I miss being a kid at Christmas,' Tara says wistfully, and I think she's psychic until I realise there's a Santa up ahead handing out something to squeaking kids.

Fee frowns. 'I don't know, isn't it weird when you think about it? Sitting on Santa's lap . . .'

'Probably a creepy old perv,' I agree, and the three of us crack up.

'Count of three,' I whisper as we get closer to Santa, and then as we're making our way around the crowd scream, 'Creepy old perv!' in unison and run off, still laughing when we get to the bus stop.

It's always weird, the things that make you bond with people, but shrieking at a man dressed as Santa is definitely one of them.

Week six, day three

Our last week of school before the Christmas holidays. We don't have exams this year, unlike the other years, so we finish a few days earlier than the rest of the school. Nevertheless that doesn't exempt us from our Christmas Mass.

There's nothing like a good Mass, right? I wish they'd just let us watch an episode of *Father Ted* instead.

The nearest church is just around the corner, so we have to walk there, even though it's raining. I am all prepared for making the journey solo, but Tara and I find ourselves falling into step together.

Tara's online profile – she added me last week – is not what I expected. It's full of links to feminist blogs and a 'fuck selfies' vibe, and I don't know why I somehow assumed that because she's pretty she'd love taking photos of herself. It reminds me of – me.

'How d'you think you get excommunicated?' she asks now, as we step around either side of a large puddle.

'I don't know,' I muse.

'We must find out. Sex with a priest, would that do it?'

'Ugh, but then you'd actually have to have sex with a priest.'

We are giggling in a most un-Christian fashion when we arrive at the church and file into one of the rows.

After a few minutes we are all hushed and the Mass begins. The priest gets up and says stuff. My mum makes a speech. I think – the same thought I've had every Christmas for the last few years – how weird it would be to be the Virgin Mary, pregnant without ever having sex. Or, you know, so she said, anyway. The utter creepiness of an angel turning up at your bedside going, *Hey, Mary, you're going to be a mammy now.*

And did she wonder? Did she count back to her last period, did they have calendars back then? Wait, they must have. I remember seeing this thing online about the earliest calendars and counting twenty-eight days and someone pointing out that who, exactly, needs to count that out? Women.

Did she count back to her last period?

Did she?

Count back.

Count back to your last period.

Count back.

And doesn't it make sense that I am sitting in the most holy of places when fear slices through me?

The priest calls an assortment of girls and teachers up for readings. Phrases drift in and out. *Lord have mercy. Christ have mercy. Lamb of God.* The responses come to me automatically, like muscle memory, even though the last time I stepped in a church was this time last year.

Amazing how often the Virgin Mary gets mentioned at Mass. How much they focus on that. Not how it felt for her or anything. Who cares, like.

119

Count back.

(It's stress.)

Count back.

(I've got the dates wrong.)

And then. The bit that usually reminds me of vampirism and cannibalism. Communion. Jesus, bread and wine. Only now when the priest says the words they feel louder, echoing in my ears.

This is my body, which will be given up for you.

And I think, so fiercely I almost leap out of my seat, so strongly Tara looks at me weirdly and mouths 'what's up?': *Fuck. That. Shit.*

Before

'Do you wanna have kids?' you ask me one day. One of the just-us days, hanging out in my room. I've shown you the latest photos of Caoilfhionn, my niece, and a video of her crawling towards Liz while Brian holds the camera and calls out encouragement.

I shrug. 'I don't know.'

'I think I do,' you say, which surprises me.

'Really?'

'Yeah. What, you don't think I'd be a good mum?'

'No, you'd be a great mum,' I say. Meaning it. I can imagine you hugging your kids. Geraldine doesn't hug you when you leave the house, the way my mum hugs me. I am big into hugging at the moment. I've been reading stuff about how if you don't get enough hugs a day you become emotionally stunted. It makes a lot of sense.

'Eh, I dunno. Might be crap.'

'Sure, might be,' I say, pretending to agree with you.

'Hey!'

'You'd be good. You like them.'

'Everyone likes kids.'

I'm not entirely convinced this is true. There are people who abuse kids, who murder them, who straight-up neglect them. 'I don't know, I don't think I do. Maybe I'm weird.'

'Well, we knew that.'

We decide when we grow up you'll have three kids – you will carry one of them and make your wife carry the other two, because it sounds pretty hideous and painful (but she's allowed to have twins to minimise the agony) – and I'll come over every second weekend to babysit and read to them. Stories about wild things and Gruffalos and caterpillars and bears who can't find their hats.

You'll be working as an important lawyer type or maybe have your own business, and I will be managing a small theatre company and teaching singing on the side (you say, knowledgeably, that people working in the arts always have at least two jobs, and I take your word for it). I won't have any kids of my own but I will be very satisfied with my career and have a String of Lovers.

'A string of them? Do I need that many?'

'It'll keep you young,' you say, laughing.

'How come you get a wife and I don't?' Even the possibility of being able to marry a woman when we grow up is new, not a thing that existed here when we were kids. How weird is that, how quickly the world can change when people want it to?

'You're not going to settle down with kids, you might as well enjoy yourself,' you say. You make it sound like 'settling down' and 'settling for' are the same thing.

Maybe I don't especially want kids but I can still have a person, can't I?

But you've already moved on to the next thing, which is the fabulous apartment I will live in, so I say nothing.

Week six, day four

It's stress.

It's stress and I'm just making it worse by stressing about the stress.

I mean, sure, we don't have exams, but there's the so-called musical and the generally icky atmosphere of school and just, well, living in the world.

And I have friends who are not talking to me.

And Justin who's not talking to me.

Not that it even matters really because I don't need Justin to talk to me, I don't need Justin for anything, there's nothing that we need to discuss.

It's stress. Teenagers are stressed. There's always things in the news about how much pressure we're under. We are a generation of over-stimulated something-or-others.

And it is easy to have deep, gasping, horror moments in the middle of a stained-glass church, where too many warm bodies and too much recitation in unison makes it feel surreal. This is what I tell myself.

This is my body –

When the phrase comes into my head at school, or at

dinner with my parents, I force myself to think about my First Communion, all of us at age eight in frilly white dresses. Baby brides.

(Not baby. No, Lauren.)

It's stress.

Week six, day five

I am not a stalker. I swear.

I am just waiting outside a certain school. A boys' school. One that Justin might attend.

Okay, fine, I'm a stalker.

It's not like I'm hovering at the front door. I'm at the bus stop across the road, possibly plausibly waiting for a bus to arrive. I'm checking my phone, held up high in front of me, and definitely not looking past it to scan the crowd of grey uniforms for blond hair and blue eyes.

In my head I practise. *Hey, can we talk? I think I might be . . .*

Or maybe he'll just look at me and see it in my eyes: something's up. He'll ask what's going on. He'll understand. Everything else will fall away because this is bigger than an ordinary break-up.

Laur, it's okay, he'll say. *We'll get through this.*

And then I see them. Cassidy first, because he's the loudest. 'Don't be homophobic, dearest!' he shrieks.

Justin to one side of him, and someone else – Kelly? – to the other.

'She's fuckin' mental,' maybe-Kelly says.

'That's so *offensive*!' Cassidy trills in his imitation of a girl voice. Well. Not any girl voice. Mine.

A thought occurs to me: if I was making fun of someone, regardless of where it was, I'd be looking around carefully, making sure they weren't there.

The three boys? They're oblivious. I watch them head off down the road together, not once glancing over to see me. Justin is laughing. He's laughing at this.

This boy who has been inside me would rather be the cool dude around his friends than be a decent human being.

Okay. Okay.

I walk home in a daze. The house is empty – parents still at work – but there is a huge stash of wine in the shed, I know – a couple of crates purchased for Christmas. Dad has some contact who gets him a really good discount.

I pick a bottle. Take it to bed with me. Panic after the first glass (a normal glass, not a proper wine glass) and go fetch another one from the shed. Just in case.

Dad's home first. Taps on my door. 'Lauren?'

'Hmm?' I say.

He opens it, notices the light's off. Just me watching rubbish on my laptop. Bottles hidden in the drawer of my bedside locker.

'In bed already?'

'Yeah. Tired.'

He nods. 'Get some rest. Night, honey.'

'Night.'

The door closes. A sigh of relief.

She's fuckin' mental . . .

Another glass.

Week seven, day one

Today's internet discovery: most pregnancies end in miscarriages. So early that most people don't know, and also people don't really talk about it when it happens before twelve weeks.

I find support forums for women who have miscarried and feel like they can't talk about it, like no one understands, and the tears roll down my cheeks in some weird kind of sympathy. Weird because I wish I could take that experience from them. Swap with them, these women who wanted babies so very badly.

These grown-ups.

I also learn – aren't personal crises so useful for the educational opportunities they provide? – that the twelve-week mark, the magical time when you're 'allowed' to tell people, when it's safe to, is not twelve weeks. It's more like ten. They don't count from conception, they count from the date of your last period. Like before it's even happened you're already this vessel-in-waiting.

Week seven, day three

I feel sort-of sick waking up again but I don't know if that's nerves or morning sickness and I don't care. What I know now is that it's Tuesday and I'm off school and Brian and Liz and Caoilfhionn will be back for Christmas tomorrow, which feels like the official start to the festive season. So it is my private deadline for my body to get back to normal.

Normal period-anticipation is about dread. The fear of wine-dark stains on your jeans or the back of your skirt or someone's couch or the bus seat. Running to the bathroom as soon as you can, or hobbling there if it feels necessary to do so to prevent epic fountains of blood. And then the gut-wrenching cramps, the sickening ache . . .

Tuesday, eleven a.m. I've been awake for four hours – why is it that during the school term it's horrendous getting up early and when it's the holidays it's so easy to be awake? Both the parents are at work. I'm itching to get out of the house. I know I need to buy a test, I know, I know, but it is so much easier said than done.

I will go talk to one of those crisis-pregnancy places, the kind that get advertised on the backs of bathroom doors in shopping centres and at the side of your screen as soon as you start searching for pregnancy-themed topics.

How responsible is that? While still putting off the inevitable.

Because I know. And I don't know how I know, and I don't buy into this mystical lady-in-touch-with-her-body thing, but I just *do*.

My sense of direction is pretty crap at the best of times, which is why I'm glad to have Google Maps, but once I'm on the right street I turn it off because it drains the battery like crazy. I don't know quite what I'm expecting as I edge past different buildings, but then the word 'abortion' flashes out at me like a neon sign, even though it's only one word in a black-and-white newspaper article in the window.

Okay. Here we go. Inside, I ask the lady at reception, an older woman in a navy cardigan with some kind of gold pin on the lapel, so grandmotherly, if there's an appointment available. She takes my details and tells me to wait.

I pull out my phone, listen to music (*The Sound of Music* soundtrack – one of my favourites), but I'm too shaky to really take any of it in, even as I skip ahead to 'I Have Confidence' in the hope that it will rub off on me. Why am I nervous? I didn't think I would be. I don't know why my hands are trembling. I don't know why I want to hug my arms tight around myself. (I haven't been getting enough hugs, I think.)

There are other women here, all youngish, though I can't really tell. A lot of them are Asian – I think Chinese or Korean, but please don't hold me to that – and could be anywhere between fifteen or forty. Some of them are white but I realise when they go up to the reception their first language is not

English, not even close. It's not the almost-perfect or often better-than-native speech of any of the Eastern European girls in my school – it's fumbling. Awkward.

I don't know why this makes me feel more afraid. I should feel superior, right? Confident with my fluency, and everything I already know from the internet. But when I go in to talk to the counsellor, similarly sensibly cardiganed, she looks at me and shakes her head. 'You're very young,' she says. 'You've got your whole life ahead of you.'

(Yes. Exactly. Isn't that the point?)

She hands me brochures. Gorgeous bouncing babies. One is about the extended family and the support they can offer young mothers. The other is about adoption services and good families who will provide a home for your child.

I let her talk for a while, out of politeness, and then she says, 'Do you have any questions for me, Lauren?'

'Um. I actually wanted – I know you can't perform it here, but I know you can give me information, so, um, I wanted to know about abortion.'

The look. The look on her face. 'All right, Lauren.' And she takes out another brochure. This one is not glossy. It is flimsy. There is a foetus on the front cover. Like, recognisably one. Almost a baby. You can make out fingers and toes. A large-headed creature curled up in the womb.

'Now, Lauren, the thing you need to understand about abortion is that the baby, at this stage, is even more sensitive than you or I would be to pain. Do you understand?' She says more, things about injections and nerves. I only take half of it in. I am still staring at the picture.

'And you're still very young, you have to think about the rest of your life. So if you were to go on to have other children, which I'm sure you will, well, we find that with women who've had this procedure, they're still carrying a lot of guilt around. So they're sometimes over-protective of their other children, or they can neglect them . . . We see a lot of abuse with these women.' She leans closer to me when she says this, imparting this confidential information.

She keeps going on about surgery and how it will increase my chances of breast cancer or how sometimes they miss and end up perforating the bowel and then you're carrying around a colostomy bag for the rest of your life.

I can't breathe. This is too fucking outrageous. My brain's telling me, *get out, Lauren, get out of here right now*, but a tiny part of me is terrified that she's being honest, just wants to give me the worst-case scenario so I *know*. Like when Brian got his wisdom teeth out and they told him they had to warn him that there was a rare paralysing thing in a bit of the jaw that could happen with the anaesthetic. It practically never happens but they had to say it all the same (it completely freaked him out, though). There are risks with every surgery.

Then I remember. 'But what if it's not surgical, what if it's a medical abortion?'

'How far along are you?' she asks, and it's then it hits me that this is the first question she should have asked me. Or, for fuck's sake, even, *are you sure*? Shouldn't there be tests?

'Um, seven weeks.' Five weeks, I think. Five weeks really.

She shakes her head sadly. 'Oh, no, you'd be too late for that.'

This is the one detail I am a hundred percent convinced I

132

am sure about without pulling out my phone to check. Maybe I haven't spent years studying this stuff and talking to loads of women like she has, maybe I haven't seen all these unexpected side-effects like she has, if she's telling the truth, but about this she is completely and utterly lying.

(Nine weeks. Up to nine weeks. That's what the websites for the clinics say. The English clinics that have special pages for Irish women because they know. They know.)

She is not wearing a name badge. Maybe she gave me her name earlier, I don't know, I've already forgotten. Heartbeat speeding up, I whip out my phone and snap a picture of her.

'What are you –' she says, taking a moment to realise I'm not just checking the time but actually photographing her.

I am too furious to talk. I slam the door behind me, and to all the girls in waiting room I say, 'Go somewhere else. They lie here. LIE.' One of the Asian girls looks up at me, alarmed. She understands, says something to the girl next to her.

'Excuse me,' the receptionist says, 'I'm afraid I'll have to ask you to –'

I'm out the door before she can say 'leave'. I snap a photo of the outside of the centre, and it's then I realise that the piece is in the window is a newspaper story about how Abortion is Evil.

I lean against the wall, shaking. I'm such an idiot. Also, I really didn't think – it's so blatant. So awful.

I look at the pictures. I want to tell the world. Share them online. Except, I realise, I can't. Posting these up under my own name in the heat of outrage might make me feel better now but in five minutes' time when people start asking, *Eh, Lauren, why were you there?* . . . everything would fall to pieces.

133

When I feel ready, I look up and down the road, wondering if there's somewhere I can sit and have a cup of tea. That's when I see it. The Family Planning Clinic. Two doors down. With proper clear signs, the kind you see outside doctor's surgeries. Even in this wretched country the genuine places don't have to hide away like that awful whatever-the-fuck-it-was.

I feel like an idiot. Partly.

The rest of me just feels exhausted, and sad, and terrified.

'Heya.'

I am sitting in a cafe near St Stephen's Green when Ellie comes over. The approach is tentative.

'How's it going?' she continues.

'Grand,' I say.

'We missed you at Q Club last weekend.'

I shrug.

'Come on, don't be sulky. Can I sit?'

'Sure.'

Q Club seems so distant. Something for a different version of me.

'I heard you had a fight with Evan,' she continues.

That fire under my skin flares up again. 'Oh, for fuck's sake, is that why you came over? To give out to me?'

'I just think you guys need to talk. You're not being fair to him, Laur. It's a really shit situation to be in.'

. . . we see a lot of abuse with these women . . .

'Gosh, I can't imagine.'

'Well –' and here I see traces of how Ellie was that day I walked out of the group – 'you *can't*, actually.'

134

I was being sarcastic, you bitch. And something inside me snaps. 'And you can't imagine what it's like to *actually* be a girl. Hating your body? Feeling trapped in it? Par for the fucking *course*, Ellie.' My voice is getting louder and louder and I know people are watching and I don't care. I don't care. I can't listen to someone who's never going to need to step into a lying-asshole-crisis-pregnancy centre ever telling me that I don't get it.

I have felt trapped in my body since I was ten years old and discovered that, contrary to the impression that Judy Blume had given me, periods were neither magical nor one-off things that happened to turn you into a woman. Every month. Every month for decades. For most of your life. The pain, the blood, the life-on-hold. The being told to get on with things because it's natural. Normal. Part of being a girl.

Get on with things. Get on with everything. Doesn't matter what it is. Just shut the fuck up and get on with it.

'You're really out of line,' Ellie says in what might be the most patronising tone I have ever heard. And I think: you might be a girl, Ellie, but you have the same body parts as the asshole guy who gets to walk away from this thing inside me, who has the luxury of not having to deal with it.

'You know what? You can fuck right off.' By now it's a proper scream. By now the whole world has faded to me and Ellie, and there is no space for me to give a shit about anything but *my* shit. I am already out the door before I realise it, breathing too fast, head spinning, suddenly understanding why and how people might run into traffic or jump off tall buildings.

I need someone and I am running out of someones.

I know it's taking a risk, but there is so much more at stake here that it barely registers. I message Fee and Tara. *Hi ladies – anyone around town right now? Need a friend (long story). L xx*

Week seven, day three (later)

Tara's down the country with her family, but Fee sends a message saying she's about ten minutes away. She must either be already in town or else on the bus. Either way I breathe a sigh of relief, feel the adrenaline in my system taper off to something resembling normal.

This is how it should be. Supportive sisterhood stuff, right? I'm always reading stuff online about how female friendships are so important and need to be nurtured. And I know, because I am not a *complete* moron (incidents involving wandering into the wrong 'clinic' aside), that this is a new, delicate friendship but it also feels like one that could withstand this.

This is the kind of thing that brings people closer together, surely? Fee's probably had a pregnancy scare before. By the time she arrives I've already imagined her entire relationship history: first boyfriend at eleven, just kissing, then onto a couple more including the seventeen year old when she was fifteen who basically expected sex so she gave it to him, and then realised it could actually be really good and fun and was a thing they did together instead of 'for' one another. Her period was late twice, but both times it was just stress, she had exams coming up, but she was scared because even though she was on the Pill she'd also been sick and that can mess it up for you.

So this is how I start, once she sits down next to me in Supermacs (nothing says intimate conversations about the contents of your womb like fast food, right?): 'Hey, have you ever had a pregnancy scare?' Because I am convinced she has.

Her eyes widen. 'What? No. *What?*'

I remind myself that I am not actually Sherlock Holmes. 'Sorry. I just –'

'I've never even – I'm a virgin.'

It's like my brain goes into auto-response mode. 'I don't actually believe in the whole concept of virginity, it's so heteronormative and patriarchal and capitalist. You know?'

Fee stares at me. 'Lauren. Save that shit for Tara. What's up? Are you –' She looks around, checks if anyone's listening. 'Are you *pregnant?*'

Hearing it said aloud by someone else – someone I'm in *school* with – makes me feel a little disconnected from my body. Like I'm watching this happen, not actually participating in it. 'Yeah. I think so. Maybe.'

'Shit.' She pauses, and then says, 'Oh, double shit, this is the guy who basically dumped you without dumping you, right?'

'No, but that's not –' I start and then stop. *That's not important*, I was going to say. But I don't know, do I, what Fee might think about that? 'I haven't done a test yet,' I say instead. 'I haven't even bought one.'

'I can do that for you,' Fee says immediately. 'I'll be back in a sec.'

She's up from the table before I have the chance to push

money into her hand. My heart starts pounding. What if she's not coming back? What if she's run off to other girls at school to tell them what a stupid slut I am? What if she's calling my mother?

Is this paranoid thinking? Well, of course it's paranoid thinking, but doesn't the world sort of teach us to be paranoid? I had safe sex with my boyfriend and still, here we are, in a fucking fast-food restaurant waiting for a girl to bring a pregnancy test, and that's 'we' in the generic sense, not 'we' in the 'you and me, baby', because this is not a baby. This is not even a foetus, not yet. It is an embryo. It is a maybe.

I pull out the brochure about abortion and its evils and I squint at that picture. I've seen it before. I know it. Google 'abortion' and it will turn up, I'm sure of it. When I search for that on my phone, the brochure hidden under the table on my lap, I find the exact same image. Only it has small print next to it. That's a picture of a foetus at twenty-four weeks.

I press my fingers firmly against my mouth because I am convinced I will cry or scream or both. How is this fair? How the hell is this fair, to lie like this? What if, what if. I think of the hypothetical I always (according to Tara) give to Mrs O'Connor: what if you're a thirteen-year-old incest victim going to a place like that? What if you don't understand, what if you don't –

Holy fuck, it's only hitting me now, I mean, really hitting me. The other women there. Immigrants with wobbly English. Easier to lie to. Easier to scare.

I have to do something. But before I can, Fee is back, with a paper bag. 'Here you go.' She slides it across the table.

'How much was it?' I say, wallet at the ready.

She waves her hand. 'Don't worry about it. My treat.' She pauses for a second. 'Um . . . Happy Christmas!'

I burst out laughing. The best, belly-aching, face-hurting kind. 'I don't know if I can accept this, Fee, you haven't even gift-wrapped it. Bit tacky, like.'

She's a little slower to respond than Evan or Ellie would be, but after a second she goes, 'Santa stole the wrapping paper. You're on his naughty list.'

'Was it that Santa we saw a couple of weeks ago? He should be on his *own* naughty list.'

Fee nods towards the bag. 'You going to take it now?'

'I think at the table might be a bit much.' I look around, identify the bathrooms. 'Okay. Aaaagh.'

'Good luck,' Fee says. 'Or – you know what I mean.'

Here I am in a toilet cubicle with black-marker graffiti about who loves who *4ever* and weird in-jokes and this is the place where it all becomes definite. I slide the box out of the bag and open it up. Two slim packages, individually wrapped. I read the instructions. Then I read them again.

The outer door swings open. 'And then she's like, no, I said seven, and I'm like, you so didn't, you liar, and she's all, I have it in my phone . . .'

I can't do this with other people around. I put the things back in the box. Shove them to the bottom of my handbag.

Maybe by the time I get home my temperamental uterus will have kicked back into regular mode, ready to send me straight to bed with cramps.

(Most pregnancies end in miscarriage. Why not this one?)

When I get back to the table, Fee is on her phone. Probably just checking messages, but the fear hits me. What if she's telling other people?

'Hey,' she says gently. 'What's the news?'

What if she thinks: *you can't kill a child, you murderer?*

She has the power to tell my mother. Or to call the police. Legal to travel. Not legal to have here. Fourteen years in prison. Can they lock you up here if they find out, even if it happens abroad? I should know this and don't. Didn't even occur to me to search for it. It sounds barbaric. But so too are places like the fake clinic with the creepy counsellor telling blatant lies. And that happened. That really holy-fucking-crap happened.

'It's fine,' I say, ignoring the way my limbs feel not quite my own, the way I don't entirely feel in control of my movements. 'Off the hook.'

She shrieks, gets up and flings her arms around me. 'Oh, thank fuck, Lauren. I was so worried.'

She says, 'Let's go do something to celebrate.'

My heart still pounding. My body not my own. I am not this girl. I am not in this position. I need to escape.

I say, 'Let's get a drink.'

You're not supposed to drink when you're pregnant. Except I already have. If I am. I don't really know. Not really.

And anyway I do not want a baby.

I have never been so sure of anything in my life. For a second I imagine it: swelling up, something growing inside you that you don't want. Everything you put into your body judged,

141

because it will either help or hinder the creature inside you. Your body not your own.

I am not giving up my body. Not for nine months. Not for anything. Not unless I decide some day in the future that it is worth it for me because I want a child.

'You look so serious,' Fee says, laughing in my ear as she comes back from the bar. 'Still a bit wobbly?'

'Yeah,' I say, accepting the beer with a smile.

We're standing in a tiny corner of an absolutely packed pub, full of people with half-Irish half-other accents, emigrants home for Christmas catching up with friends. Around us we're hearing about the different prices of things in London and the sights of Vancouver and how hard you have to work in New York. The bar staff are overwhelmed, too busy to ask either of us for ID. When we first came in I had a tiny disloyal bit of relief that Tara wasn't with us: she looks much younger than us.

'You must be so relieved,' she says, not for the first time since we arrived.

'Yeah,' I say, and I almost believe it, because the beer is making things distant and I can forget that I live in a strange country where sixteen-year-olds can get hormones to change their sex but not ones to stop a pregnancy.

(But pregnant girls are just asking for trouble, aren't they? This is what happens when you have sex. Dirty whore. Accept the consequences, you tramp.)

'Well, then, cheer up!'

My head's all over the place. 'Sorry.' I push the thoughts away. To the distant place that beer can push them to. 'And thank you so much for today, seriously.'

She smiles shyly. 'Hey, we do these things for our friends.'

I smile back, feeling warm and fuzzy. 'Okay, so tell me a thing. When you came to our school, you started hanging out with – like, I don't want to say *cool girls*, because that makes us sound like we're twelve, but –'

She laughs. 'I know what you mean. They're not really my type, but – they're okay, but we don't have a lot in common.'

'So . . .'

'Well, they were the only ones who talked to me the first day. You know? So, of course I was going to be friends with them. But now with the musical and getting to know other people . . .' She shrugs.

'Wow,' I say, and realise I feel guilty. 'The rest of us are awful. Like, we should've introduced ourselves, or something, but . . .'

She waves it away. 'People have their own stuff going on. I mean, you at the start of the year . . .' She grins.

'Me what?' I can't believe she noticed anything about me.

'Okay. So remember when you said you had a boyfriend?'

'Stop bringing that up! So awkward!' I shriek.

She acknowledges this with a nod. 'Yeah, totally. But I was actually surprised, because it was so obvious you were madly in love with, oh, what's-her-name, Steph.'

'Evan,' I correct, on autopilot.

'Oh, sorry, I thought –'

The beer makes me do expansive gestures. 'It's a whole thing. Steph in school 'cause her – his – mum won't let him change his name officially, but yeah, it's a whole thing.'

'Well, that completely clears it up,' Fee says brightly.

'Evan is trans. He's a boy. Basically.'

'Except a girl.'

'Yeah. Well. Kinda. There's all these different ways of talking about it, like *identified as female at birth*, or you could be non-binary so you don't identify with either, or . . .'

Fee stares at me. 'Jesus. I need to get you and Tara to teach me stuff. I feel like such an idiot around you two, you're so, like . . . I've led such a sheltered life.'

I shrug. It's weird being around someone who doesn't think about this stuff. I mean, obviously Justin and his friends didn't, but they're guys. I didn't expect them to. But girls . . . 'The thing is, we all do things that fit into some stereotype or other. Like, we're drinking beer, not cocktails, which is macho. But also have long hair, so feminine.'

'You think too much,' Fee says. Accurately.

'Yeah.'

'But it's kinda cool. I like it.'

'Oh my God,' I say suddenly, because I have the best idea. 'D'you wanna play a game?'

She looks wary. 'What kind of game?'

I realise my beer's almost gone. 'I'll get us more and then explain.'

At the back of my head I know I shouldn't be spending money on booze when I need to save for the thing that I will need to travel to do, but also. Also beer.

'Okay,' I say when I come back. 'Me and Steph used to play this all the time.' I realise the slip as soon as I've said it. Easier to catch yourself when sober. 'You look at anything in a room and then decide whether it's feminist or problematic. That's it. So, like . . . beer. Is it empowering and feminist that we're

144

drinking it, as women, smashing gender stereotypes about beverage choices? Or is it problematic because . . .'

'Because these bottles are really phallic,' Fee jumps in.

I stare at her. 'I'm so proud of you right now.'

She beams. 'Okay, let's see. This coaster. Feminist or problematic?'

I ponder. 'It's circular, so, like, curvy?'

'So kinda feminist, saying you don't need to have a perfect body shape, that women have curves,' Fee continues. She's really getting into it.

'But is that a reductive way of looking at women?'

'Oh my God, you're right! And it's advertising a lager, which promotes alcohol abuse, so I would say definitely problematic.'

'Ladies,' a twenty-something guy says from behind us, and I turn around. He is slightly swaying. 'Can I just say, you two are the best-looking women in the whole place here.'

'You can certainly,' I say, 'and I believe you just did.'

'Do you mind me asking . . .' he begins.

'Oh, I do, actually,' I reply cheerfully, and then turn back to Fee.

'Problematic,' she mouths, and we crack up.

By the time it's dark out the bar staff have changed shifts and the new guys won't serve us without ID, and anyway we are both a little wobbly. Home on the bus, packed full of people, and there is much hugging when I get off at my stop.

Approaching home, the butterflies start up, only partly quelled by the beer still in my system. I find a roll of mints in my handbag and chew three of them all together, but I worry that they'll know I've been drinking. Properly drinking, not just having a supervised glass of wine.

145

The fear, the fear, but then – no cars in the driveway. I check my phone and it's still early enough – just after six – but it's Christmas week. Why are they working late this week? 'Workaholics,' I declare to the empty house.

I head up to my room, throw my bag on the floor, and try to not think about what's at the bottom of it, two plastic-wrapped wands ready to make everything real.

Week seven, day four

Four a.m. That's the time my phone tells me. I'm wide awake, thirsty as hell, and once I go downstairs to fetch a bottle of water I know I just have to do it now.

It's not a surprise, when the second line shows up, a bit before the three-minute window is up. I watch it darken in colour.

It's not a surprise. Which doesn't mean that it's not a *shock*.

I watch *Dirty Dancing* and cry.

I listen to the *Spring Awakening* soundtrack and cry.

I research online, revisiting sites I've already read, making sure it's all clear in my head. I could order pills and take them at home, which is supposed to be safe, but then I read about Customs seizing packages of medication and how it's illegal to import drugs and I cry.

I am losing a lot of liquid today.

I can only do one scary thing today. This is what I have decided. A little bargain with myself.

When Mum and Dad go to work – it's still early in the morning, I haven't been able to get back to sleep – I call the first clinic in England. I get an answering machine, which is just as well, because my mouth has gone too dry to say anything.

I don't leave a message. What would I say?

Okay. Phone calls are too much right now. I wish there was just a button to click, an online booking system.

Instead I open up a Word document and type up as much as I can remember from the 'clinic'. The address. What that lady said. The other women there. I take photos of the different leaflets, and pull up that twenty-four-week foetus picture as well. Transfer yesterday's photos to my computer.

I am surprised how easy it is to find journalists' email addresses. I find ones – almost all women – who have written pro-choice articles in the last year. I stare at one for a while, a woman who's written about her experience terminating a pregnancy that wasn't going to survive more than a day or two.

No. Not her. She is too like the women on the miscarriage support forums. She would judge me. She would hate me.

I set up a new email address. I am no longer Lauren Carroll. I am Irish Girl.

I send them everything I have. The words, the photos.

Please do something about this, I type. *Please.*

Before

Last summer, just after our exams are finished, we get pleasantly tipsy and decide it is a good idea to have a sleepover. Like we used to all the time before we discovered drinking and Q Club and parties with lots of people.

We stay over at your place, because Geraldine hasn't the slightest idea that you might be into girls, whereas my mother knows that I go to Q Club and like girls sometimes and has taken to saying 'I'll make up the bed in the guest room' when I mention you staying over.

Sometimes we talk about this: how weird it is to be expected to 'come out', which is basically going 'hey, here's who I want to have sex with'. Is that ever a conversation anyone wants to have with their parents? And you only have to do it if you're not straight.

We are not talking about this tonight.

We are not really talking much about anything.

You are on a high from finishing the exams of doom, and I know you'll have done brilliantly, and all I can think is how beautiful you look and how much I want –

I want everything.

My mouth is on yours and we've done this before but there's something different here. Lasting longer. More intense.

I'm unbuttoning your shirt.

You're sliding your fingers underneath my top.

At some point we look at each other – is this really happening? – but it's also so, so, what's the word? So inevitable. This has been coming for a long, long time.

I step out of my jeans. I shrug off my top. I am standing here in my bra and knickers, and you're touching me, and eventually those come off too, because they're just getting in the way, really, aren't they? And standing is inconvenient angle-wise so I fall back down onto the bed next to you.

When you slip one, then two fingers inside me, I make a sound that makes you laugh and say, 'Shhh!', but your eyes are burning holes into mine and you stay looking dead at me while you move. While you make me gasp. While you do the thing to me that I've never experienced with another person and I didn't know how intense that could be – not just the physical rush, but that intimacy.

Your eyes burning holes into mine.

You. You. You.

Week seven, day four (later)

'Hey, kiddo,' Brian says, ruffling my hair.

'Hey, oldie,' I reply, sticking out my tongue.

'Hey, darling, lovely to see you,' Liz says, offering up a hug. She holds me at arm's length. 'You're looking fabulous.'

At least she didn't say I was *glowing*. I like Liz. I don't know her that well but she treats me like a person and not just Annoying Little Sister, which is always nice.

'Give your Auntie Lauren a kiss,' she instructs Caoilfhionn, who's clinging to her side.

Caoilfhionn shakes her head, holds on to Liz's trouser leg even more tightly.

'Go on, don't be shy!' Brian says.

'It's okay,' I say quickly. It has just hit me how creepy this is. A kiss, or a hug – something to be offered up willingly, not ordered to provide. 'How was your flight?'

'Flights plural,' Brian says.

Liz nods. 'I'm wrecked.' She doesn't look it, but she gives a huge yawn like she's trying to prove her point. 'This little one slept through the whole thing, though.'

'Do you guys want a cup of tea or something?' It's weird

playing hostess to your own brother, but that's what I do: put the kettle on, make tea and coffee and set out biscuits for the three of them in the living room, where the Christmas tree now proudly sits, having been dragged down from the attic. We used to get a real one every year when I was a kid, until the parentals decided it was too much work. Now it's a matter of dusting off the fake decorated tree once it's downstairs rather than adorning a real one.

I fetch a couple of my old picture books from the spare room, and let Caoilfhionn turn the pages of them as she sits on the floor. She doesn't have a clue what the words are, but she really likes turning the pages. We've been sent various videos of this happening over the past few months.

'She's so funny,' Liz says fondly.

. . . *we see a lot of abuse with these women* . . .

'Yeah,' I say.

I hear about how work is going and how great the beaches are and how much better it is in Melbourne than Dublin.

'What are you doing next summer?' Liz wants to know. 'If you can get away, do, seriously, it's so good to take advantage of the summer holidays at your age.'

I shrug. 'I don't know. I'll probably go away with the parents, I don't think they'd let me off on my own yet.'

The irony of this is not lost on me, no.

'Ah, they should! You'll be nearly seventeen then, won't you?'

'Yeah, but you know what they're like. They'd let me go on something organised, though, I suppose. If it was educational.' I think about Ellie's nerd camp, about songwriting camp. There must be some kind of residential programme I could do. I am

152

pretty sure I have read books about musical theatre summer camps. Or maybe I dreamt that.

'There's a crowd that do a coding workshop for teenagers,' Brian says in what I think is an attempt to be helpful. 'One of my friends from college works there.'

'Cool,' I say, even though doing coding is just not my kind of thing.

Silence then, and Caoilfhionn comes up to me and pokes me with one of the books. She clambers on top of me, heavier than she looks, and I put my arms around her and read the book to her, doing all the voices.

'You're so good with her,' Liz says.

I'm not, really. I am good with things like this: performing a story. I don't know what else to do with kids. But it's supposed to be instinctive.

There is a part I am missing. Something broken inside me.

'Hey,' I say after dinner, when it's just me and Brian loading up the dishwasher, and Mum and Dad are busy cooing over Caoilfhionn like they've never seen a tiny child before (jealousy stabs at me a little bit, even though I know that's ridiculous). 'Can I ask you a really big favour?'

This is weird. There is too much of an age gap between us for there to be a shared childhood history. In my earliest memories, Brian's already in his late teens, old enough to think I'm cute rather than to be annoyed by me. Too old to ever see me as an equal. He'll probably still treat me like a kid when I'm forty.

'You can ask, sure,' he says, grinning. 'Doesn't mean I'll say yes.'

I roll my eyes. 'So there's a couple of really good gigs coming up and tickets are going on sale soon and I really want to go, but I'm really broke. Is there any chance you'd lend me the money? I'll pay you back with pocket money and stuff, it's just they're the kind of things you really need to book as soon as they go on sale . . .'

'How much d'you need, a couple of hundred?'

'Yeah. Three hundred, if you have it.' This is as much as I feel like I can reasonably ask for, under this pretext. I cross my fingers.

He lets out a whistle. 'Jesus, ticket prices are mental these days, aren't they?'

'Yeah, I know.'

'Listen, did you ask the parents about it, are they being stingy?'

What does it say about my scheming mind that I have an answer ready for this? 'Oh my God, no, not at all. But they've been paying for loads of TY stuff, trips and extra stuff, so I don't want to ask them for more, you know?'

He nods. 'Yeah. Transition Year's a real racket in some places, isn't it?'

'Tell me about it,' I say.

He looks like he's weighing it up. 'Yeah, okay, I need to double-check with Liz, but we can probably manage three hundred.'

'Seriously?'

'Yeah, seriously,' he says.

I can't remember the last time I've hugged Brian properly – not the dutiful quick squeeze at airports, but proper bear hugs.

But now I do. 'You're the best.' Dangerously close to crying here.

He shuffles, looks kind of embarrassed. Yeah. We don't really do hugs.

'I'll pay you back . . .' I start.

'Ah, no, we'll call it your Christmas present,' he says.

Is it terrible that I was hoping he'd say that? That instead of feeling the gratitude I know I should, all that's trickling through me is a faint sense of relief?

Week seven, day five

You know what's really hypocritical? Cis gay girls refusing to accept that you're trans while they're running around with their pretend boyfriends acting like they're straight so they'll fit in with the cool girls. TALK ABOUT DENIAL!!!

I stare at Evan's post. I mean, where do I begin? The smug, self-righteous comments on it, or the fact that it's online at all?

I type 'you are a pathetic child' and then delete. Because that in itself would be pathetic. But I'm furious.

Which is deliberate. I can do this if I'm angry. I have spent my morning looking for things to make me angry.

I pick up the phone and I call the first clinic, who can't fit me in until school starts back. I try another one. The third time is the charm. An appointment the first week of January. I will pay in cash.

This is what I'm doing while all you guys are being assholes online, I think. Living in the real world. Everything else feels like it's all on the other side of a very thick pane of glass, an airplane window maybe. No hope of smashing through it even if you went at it with a hammer.

Airplane window. Airplanes. I need to book flights.

My dad's business card is off-limits, even though that would be the logical one to use for travel expenses. He's always going on about how accountancy firms are the absolute worst for cross-checking absolutely every little detail on work cards, even when it's something tiny like a cup of coffee during a business meeting.

His personal credit cards live in his wallet, which lives in his pocket or else is left on his bedside locker at night. And the thought of creeping into my parents' bedroom in the middle of the night is unsettling on two counts. One, they might catch me. Two, I might catch them in the middle of an activity I can intellectually understand they might still get up to but emotionally really don't need to know about.

Mum, on the other hand, leaves her wallet in her handbag, usually left on the kitchen counter overnight. I sit through dinner – all of us cooing over Caoilfhionn the whole time – and then go and hide in my room until everyone's gone to bed. Brian and Liz are out for the night, catching up with old friends, with Mum and Dad on babysitting duty. I hear voices and murmurings and laughter and put on some music to block it out. Soundtrack from *The Book of Mormon*. It is about the most ridiculous and distracting thing I can think of.

Finally, finally, everyone is in bed. Not a creature is stirring, except for me. I tiptoe down the steps. Enter the kitchen. Put the kettle on to boil, just so I have an excuse if I need one.

Mum's handbag is practical and huge, a giant brown leather thing that she got in the sales a few years ago. Anything you could ever want – plasters, cough drops, tampons, painkillers, nasal spray – lives somewhere in here.

The wallet is in a zipped pocket. I take it out, my ears attuned to any sound from upstairs. There are two credit cards, one debit. I slide each out in turn, and take photos of the front and back – number and security code – with my phone.

I check the various folds of the wallet, but the other cards are loyalty cards for supermarkets or gift cards for department stores.

There's a creak from over my head and I freeze. Nothing else happens, but it has me nervous all the same. I replace everything, switch off the kettle, and retreat to my bedroom.

There is one card more familiar than the others, the black-and-blue credit card. I have a flash – or maybe I'm only imagining it – of seeing it pulled out for groceries or clothes. The more things appearing on a credit card statement, the less anyone might notice a particular item. And I don't even think Mum looks at her statements that carefully. She has a direct debit set up; the bill is paid automatically. (These are the things you talk about at dinner when you have an accountant dad.)

I check the flight times, book myself in for an early-morning and a late-night to and from Liverpool. It's a short flight. In rush-hour traffic it would take longer to get from one side of Dublin to the other.

Week seven, day seven

Christmas Eve: my parents go to Midnight Mass, which despite the name actually takes place at ten o'clock. Brian, Liz, Caoilfhionn and I watch the first three *Star Wars* movies (as in episodes four, five and six – no wonder mathematical ability is declining if this is how counting goes), which is to say that Caoilfhionn plays with her toys and the three of us share a couple of bottles of wine.

'When's Santa coming?' Caoilfhionn asks several hundred times. When we pause the DVD and Brian brings her up to bed – the three of them are in the spare room – I tell Liz the story of how Brian destroyed Christmas for me.

'So I'm like, six, and he's eighteen, and I want – oh, I don't know, some kind of baby karaoke thing, and I'm going on about how I hope Santa notices how hard I've been trying to be *really good*, and he looks at me and goes, "You know Santa's not real, right?"'

Liz shrieks. 'Oh, no, he didn't! The brat!'

'And I'm there with these big eyes like it can't possibly be true, and I say, "No, Santa's real!" and he just says, "You're such a baby."' I'm laughing now, after wine, but I remember being so upset at the time. Everyone else at school still believed in Santa one hundred percent. There was never any question of doubting the magic.

'Oh no, you poor creature!'

'I know! So it's Christmas morning, and I turn to the parents and go, "Did you buy the Santa presents?"'

'You didn't.'

'I did! I'm holding a doll or something and I ask them, and my dad kind of mumbles and says, "Don't be silly," and my mum goes, "Does it matter where they came from?"'

Liz groans. 'Such a giveaway. I can so see your mam saying that, though.'

'I know! So we get into this really existential crisis thing about the meaning of gifts, and then Dad goes, "Just don't tell anyone at school," and there you go, there's my childhood crushed.' Wine makes me melodramatic.

'Oh, Lauren.'

For a moment I think: this is it. This is my person, my sister-in-law, this is the person I tell. This is the woman who will understand. Who will hug me (we need hugs). Who will stroke my hair and squeeze my hand and tell me that everything's going to be okay. This is maybe the woman who will say, *before Brian, before Caoilfhionn, there was a situation* . . . and she will know it was the right thing to have done.

I open my mouth. And then Brian's back, and we're unpausing the DVD, and Liz takes the piss out of him for destroying the Santa-myth for me, and soon enough the parents are back from Midnight Mass with tales of how great the choir were, and it's all too normal and real-life to interrupt with this thing. This bigness.

160

By the time the movie ends I'm ready to fall asleep. 'Night!' I say cheerfully, and it doesn't feel like Christmas Eve. I am no longer excited about what Santa might bring. I just want it to be the first week of January. I just want to be able to breathe again.

Week eight, day one

Caoilfhionn is jumping on my bed. Including on my legs. A strangled noise emerges from my mouth.

'Caoilfhionn, honey, don't be bothering your Auntie Lauren,' Liz says, mouthing 'sorry' over her head from the doorway.

'It's fine,' I mumble, because that's what you're supposed to do.

'Chriiiiistmas! Santy!'

If I ever have kids, I think, I'm not doing the whole Santa thing.

Then I remember and it's like a cold shower.

Downstairs, this is definitely The Caoilfhionn Show. She tugs inexpertly at the wrapping paper on all the presents, not limiting herself to her own, and Mum and Dad and Brian and Liz coo over how adorable she is, and I want to go back to bed and sleep for another couple of hours.

I remember getting excited about presents, but now I open them with a sense of panic. Thank you very much, Auntie Maeve and Uncle Gerry for the lovely gift set of bath stuff, and I'm not even going to take offence like I would have a few years ago and presumed it was a hint to go wash myself, but couldn't you have given me, oh, *money*?

Card from Brian and Liz with a 'P.S. Check your bank account!' I already checked last night and know he's transferred the money. But still. I smile and say thank you and hug them both and then Caoilfhionn leaps in and pokes me in the eye. Which at least gives me an opportunity to excuse myself on account of the watering eye and go have a quick cry in my bedroom.

Card from Paula, Dad's much-younger sister who resists the Auntie title, and my heartbeat speeds up and then slumps back to normal when I see that she's included a gift card rather than cash.

Which I know is terribly thoughtful and all and people think cash is such an impersonal gift, but when you're sixteen and don't have much money of your own it's the best thing you could ever give someone.

I tell myself I will remember this if I ever have –

Stop it, Lauren.

'That's the last of them,' Dad announces, even as Brian is reliving his childhood and crawling under the tree to see if we've missed anything. He gathers up the wrapping paper for the recycling bin. Another year of Christmas presents done.

I excuse myself again and lock my bedroom door behind me. My phone will distract me, or at least I think it will, but there are only the most generic group Happy Christmas messages awaiting me. The most personal one is from Fee – *Hey Lauren, happy happy Xmas! xxx* – and even then it doesn't feel enough. Nothing is enough.

I miss having a *person*.

Hey J, hope you're having a fab Christmas. Miss you. L xxx

Yes. Yes. I am an idiot. As soon as I've sent it I want to block out the memory of it. Forget what a mess everything is.

Week eight, day two

When I wake up it's dark outside. My phone says three a.m.

I am still in my Christmas outfit, a black skirt and baggy top, still have my cheesy reindeer necklace around my neck.

A flash: Christmas dinner. Dad saying, 'Lauren, take it easy,' as I top up my wine. Dessert, into the living room to watch something on TV. What, I have no idea. Mum saying, 'No, pet, you've had enough.' Me storming out of the house in a huff.

(Oh fuck.)

Brian – it must've been Brian – telling me to cop on and come back inside. Some petrol station. Did I walk that far? The nearest petrol station is at least fifteen minutes away.

Then nothing.

Christmas is gone. Done. Finished.

Inevitably there's a Talk. Both the parents take it upon themselves to say to me, separately, variations of 'Lauren you were in a dreadful state yesterday you really need to be careful and I know it's Christmas but really I don't want to see you like that ever again do you understand?'

I nod and try to look appropriately contrite and I suppose I am, in some ways, but mostly I'm relieved that I didn't at some point announce, 'Hey, family, I'm pregnant!'

I can handle anything once it's not that.

Week eight, days three to seven

What I Do on my Christmas Holidays.

One: empty my savings account of all remaining birthday money and occasional-babysitting-gig money.

Two: invent a day trip to Cork that Q Club are going on next week. Google cultural and historical things of significance in the area to help make it sound convincing.

Three: ask Dad for money to pay for the trip. Put folded-up notes into wallet, feeling shaky and guilty.

Four: politely refuse a lift into town to get the bus to Cork, on account of how I won't actually be getting any bus.

Five: think about it and realise it will be cheaper and quicker to get the bus to the airport from town than from home and agree to said lift.

Six: check phone constantly. No response from Justin. Not that I am really expecting one. But still. Why doesn't he realise that there's something up?

Seven: start endless messages to Evan. Delete all of them because I realise they are really for Steph, not this stranger.

Eight: strategically hide bottles of beer and wine and vodka and peach schnapps (ew, tastes like nail-varnish remover smells;

can only be consumed if mixed with something else) in my bedroom, depleting an overflowing Christmas-booze supply one bottle at a time. Example: lots of relatives come over on St Stephen's Day to see Brian and Liz and Caoilfhionn before they head off to Galway to see Liz's family over New Year's. Many fancy bags with bottles left in the kitchen. One or two or three will not be missed.

Nine: consume several of these bottles, on own in bedroom, on account of both the parental units keeping an eagle eye on my alcohol consumption. Wine spritzers rather than wine are handed to me when appropriate. Tea or coffee rather than another glass offered after food consumed. That sort of thing.

Merry Christmas, everyone.

I know what it might seem like to an outsider but alcohol is the only thing that sends me back to sleep after the dreams.

In one of them I am being chased by people from school, all insisting that I'm in trouble and that the police are looking for me. The corridors are longer and more twisted than they are in real life, with corners to hide in – but eventually they catch me and handcuff me. Fee testifies in court that she bought a pregnancy test for me and the judge, who is half a stranger and half Mrs O'Connor, says that I have to go to jail.

In another one I have a flat stomach – flatter than it is now, flatter than it's ever been, probably – but the shape of a tiny hand pushes out from my belly, visible beneath the skin, like something out of a horror movie. Everyone can see it, even if I'm wearing clothes over it. That tiny hand keeps announcing itself.

Or I'm strapped to an operating table, unable to move, and a surgeon is slicing me open, and I'm pretty sure the background characters in this scenario are actually out of *Grey's Anatomy*. Then Imelda and Ann-Marie come in and pray for the poor child and decide to call her Baby Hope. (I later realise this is heavily inspired by reading about a true story. Which I need to stop doing at bedtime. But. I can't help myself.)

So I can either stay up all night sweating, my heart pounding in my chest, or I can put some music on and have a drink and eventually fall asleep, and it's not like sleeping late is a problem over the holidays. It's practically expected.

And at the back of my mind, of course it's there: maybe this will take care of it so I don't have to make that trip next week. Maybe this will solve everything.

I am living in hope. Or denial. One or the other.

Before

You. You. You.

'Your turn,' I say after a few moments, still breathing heavily, still not quite believing this is really happening.

I kiss you. I suck your fingers, tasting of me, and you let out a little whimper that thrills me.

Your shirt off. I move my hands over your breasts and wonder about appropriate lengths of time for foreplay, but then you're bucking your hips up and I'm sliding my fingers inside –

Oh holy fuck this is you, this is you, Steph, and I just want to make you come, I just want to see your head slam back onto the pillow and your mouth open in wonder – is that too porn-star-cliché-ish? Oh I don't care and I don't know and I can hardly think because this isn't about thinking, it's about skin and wet and animal sounds.

And then suddenly you jerk away. 'No. I can't.'

I stop. 'Hey. What's wrong?' Did I do something? Did I mess this up?

'I can't, I can't,' you say, and you pull your shirt back on again, wrap it around you, pull your knees up to your chest.

'Steph. Steph. It's okay. It's okay.' I put a hand tentatively on your shoulder. That seems to be welcome, so eventually I edge closer and closer to you until I'm holding you and I can feel you trembling.

There's something going on and I don't know what it is, but it terrifies the shit out of me.

Week nine, day two

Going through security I forget that I have a water bottle in my handbag, which a surly guy in uniform throws out. It is unreasonable to be irritated by this but I am.

The airport is ridiculously crowded at this hour of the morning. It's so early, still the Christmas holidays for schools, but everyone here seems to be on their way to work of some kind. Plenty of people in suits. On laptops, reading newspapers, shuffling through Important Documents. I buy a hot chocolate and find a seat where I can keep an eye on those huge screens that will shortly reveal what gate to go to.

Helpful internet told me last night – insomniac and scrolling through statistics, in between checking to see if Justin had replied to a last-chance 'can we talk?' message – there's between ten and twelve of us a day, making this journey. You'd go early in the morning, wouldn't you? This is the second flight to Liverpool out of Dublin today. Maybe someone was on that crazy-early 6.20 a.m. one. Someone else on a flight to London Gatwick. London Heathrow. Birmingham. The chances of someone else being on this flight are not unreasonably slim. Or at least someone else being in the airport right now.

I watch women travelling alone. Most of them smartly dressed, carrying laptop bags. Off to meetings, not to clinics. One in jeans with a backpack, not the super-bulky kind that you'd use for hiking and Seeing the World, just an ordinary one you might wear to school. She has red hair in a ponytail, a freckled face. I decide she's a college student in her last year of medicine, knowing she has years' more training to go before she's ready to have kids. The father is also a medical student, in the same year as her, but she gets better grades than he does, which he doesn't like.

Stop being stupid, Lauren.

I put my earbuds in and let the rest of the world fade away, until a sudden surge of people around me reminds me to check the board. Not my gate, not yet. I wander around the bookshop, walk past all the brightly coloured spines neatly lined up. Most of these are what Mum and Dad call Guilty Pleasures. Romance or thrillers. I read the back covers without taking in anything.

I've never been on a plane on my own before. I keep waiting for someone to stop me. *Young lady, where's your parent and/ or guardian?* But it doesn't happen. Not as I head towards the gate, striding along like I'm super-confident and busy and make journeys like this every day. Not as I wait in the queue, my passport and boarding card in hand. And not when the flight attendant checks my seat number and nods, and I want him to be a woman instead, who would maybe see, who would maybe think.

Middle seat. I hate the middle seat. To my left, there's a woman maybe in her thirties reading a book; to my right, a middle-aged man reading the newspaper. And there's hardly any space, with their elbows on the armrests, so I scrunch myself up. Shoulders hunched. Arms folded in, hugging myself. And still I feel like I'm taking up too much room. The woman sighs heavily a few times both before and after take-off. I can't tell whether she wants me to apologise for some perceived wrong, or to ask her what's up and sympathise with how terrible flying is.

Maybe another day I would. Or I'd snap my head towards her and say, 'Do you *mind*?' And I would turn to Mr Newspaper over on the other side and say, 'Seriously, we have absolutely no space here, you know you can read that from a tablet, right? And maybe not squash everyone else?'

Another day. Today I sit and close my eyes and listen to music, and manage not to snap at the flight attendant who taps me on the shoulder to make sure I'm listening to the safety announcements and then the other one who wants to see if I need anything to drink (for an inflated price) and then yet another one who tries to sell me a scratch card. All in the space of forty minutes.

When we begin our descent, as helpfully announced by the pilot – like we couldn't tell from the swooping feeling in our stomachs – a baby up in the front of the cabin starts to howl.

Taxis are easiest. That's what the website said, that's what the lady on the phone said. Gave me an estimated price and everything. I get sterling out of the ATM in the airport, hoping that the exchange rate has stayed the same since I checked last night, that there hasn't been some major financial crisis that'll make my euros worthless.

The driver is an older man, silvery hair, grandfatherly. There is a flicker of recognition in his eyes when I read off the address from my phone. I imagine him flinging me out. Telling me to go home. Telling me I'm a tramp, a slut, a whore, a murderer.

'God love ya,' he says in what I think must have been an Irish accent decades ago.

I can't say anything until he drops me off. Then I hand over the money. 'Thanks,' I mumble.

Here we go.

The waiting room has cream walls. A few out-of-date magazines to read. And dead silence.

The girl from the airport, the redheaded potential medical student, is not here. But there is a girl around the same age. Dark-haired, dark-eyed, reading on a Kindle and looking all zen until I look closer and see that her hands are trembling slightly. And then the two other women are closer to Mum's age. Adults.

There is so much tension in this room, so much hovering in the air. I want to break it, but what the hell do I know? I'm just a kid. I have never felt so young in my life. Maybe they'll yell at me, demand to know why a perfectly healthy teenager won't carry a child to term. Maybe they all have those reasons that the newspapers list as the acceptable ones. Rape. Incest. Fatal foetal abnormalities. That must be the case for those older women. They know the foetus won't survive. They're being kind, not selfish like me.

Another two women arrive. Somewhere in between the college-age student and the proper grown-ups. 'Go on, sit

175

yourself down there,' one directs the other. Blue eyes, long hair so perfectly white it must be dyed. I realise she is the friend who has come along to be supportive, and immediately something in my heart stings. I could live with Justin ignoring my messages, and me, if I had a friend here.

'Right,' White Hair says to the room, and the Dublin accent sets me at ease, 'who wants a cup of tea?'

The entire atmosphere lightens. Tea or coffee? Milk or sugar? These are easy questions, easy conversation topics. White Hair goes back and forth from a giant hot-water canister in the corner, runs out to the reception to ask about milk, generally minds us. Someone else comes along and mistakes her for staff.

The college-age girl never gives us her name but she tells us she's studying history at Trinity, has exams after Christmas. She's in her final year, doing a dissertation on something to do with medieval women and literacy, which apparently means mostly nuns.

'Ugh,' I say without meaning to, and she cracks up.

'Yeah, I know, but they're the only ones in that era who could actually read. Nuns and a couple of mad wealthy types.'

'I had nuns in school,' one of the older women chimes in. She's wearing a long black dress, her dark hair flowing loose. When I look at the crinkles around her eyes I realise she must dye her hair. I contemplate investigating whether there's a link between hair dye and attending abortion clinics. 'Awful bitches.'

'Ah, sure the whole system's cracked,' White Hair says.

The other older woman sniffs disapprovingly, ostentatiously, but says nothing. She turns the pages of her magazine very precisely, so precisely that I suspect she's not even reading it.

History Girl, White Hair, Black Dress and I exchange amused looks.

I find out that White Hair is a writer and actress, which I guess explains the confidence, and that Black Dress loves the theatre and is 'fierce impressed altogether' with anyone who can get up on stage. I talk to White Hair's friend, a woman in a tracksuit with big dark circles under her eyes, about music, but not about the fact that we're doing a musical in school. And then I am called in.

Appointment number one. The consultation and pill number one. Before the doctor can even start I say, 'We were using condoms, I'm not the kind of idiot who chances it.'

She grins. 'That's good to know.'

I leave feeling lighter, even though nothing's happened yet. I need to come back this afternoon for the second pill. Walking back out, I awkwardly smile at the others. And then out into the world to distract myself for a few hours.

I should've asked the others what they were doing, I realise. But there's a big difference between bonding with people in a waiting room and going for coffee with them.

I look up at tall redbrick buildings, then yellow-grey ones, all stately like only Very Important Things happen there. Liverpool reminds me of London. Maybe there's just a classic English-city model.

And then I spy it. Starbucks. Hot chocolate. There is something reassuring about the familiarity in this unfamiliar place. I check out the prices of the big Beatles exhibition on my phone, just to see, and even though it's not that expensive it hurts to look at prices for Children (5–16 years).

Children. Right.

I scroll through my contacts. Mum's number. My fingers hover over the green phone icon. But already my throat is tightening.

I send a message instead: *Arrived safe in Cork!*

She replies with a *Great, have fun.*

The full stop at the end feels like a slap. 'Have fun' is a wish with exclamation points. It should be.

Mother Dearest am actually in Liverpool waiting to have an abortion. I don't send this, obviously. But I do type it, and stare at the words until they become meaningless.

Before

There's something going on and I don't know what it is, but it terrifies the shit out of me.

You won't tell me what it is.

'Can you just go?' you say quietly, after a long silence.

'Okay,' I say. I am too worried about you to be hurt, at that moment. The hurt doesn't hit until the next day, when you haven't replied to any of my 'are you okay?' messages and then suddenly I'm bruised all over.

This isn't how it was supposed to go. We were supposed to be happy and giddy and hand-holding. This is not how the fantasy should have played out, and I have no idea what I've done wrong. How I've ruined everything.

Week nine, day two (later)

I discover that apparently most people don't ask follow-up questions about the not having sex for two weeks after an abortion (and also to remember that you can get pregnant quite soon after, so to Be Careful) such as, 'But that's just about penetration, right? You can still masturbate if you're not, like, going in?'

In my defence this was less about being horny and more about the cramp-helping qualities of orgasms, because there is much bleeding on the way. Like a super-super-heavy period. Joy!

My handbag has numbers and information about post-abortion care, about where to go or who to talk to if you have All the Feelings or if anything goes wrong. I have been reassured that it's okay to tell an Irish doctor that you were pregnant, tell them you had a miscarriage. If there are complications, do seek help. Don't close your eyes and hope it all goes away.

When the doctor sees my face she says, 'You'll probably be fine, Lauren. This is just in case, okay?'

This is not fear on my face. This is – I don't know. Incredulity. What medieval backwater am I heading back to?

'Lauren?' she says, gently.

It spills out of me before I realise it's coming. 'Why the – why the fucking *fuck* am I not in a clinic in Dublin right now?' A bus ride away from my bed instead of a sea away?

The look on her face. The pity. The rage. The powerlessness.

'I'm sorry,' she says, squeezing my shoulder gently.

Me too.

The taxi driver heading back to the airport is proper Liverpudlian. He tells me about his holiday in Bulgaria – 'cheap as chips'. He asks if I've been out to various pubs and clubs and says, 'All work and no play makes Jack a dull boy.' I am pretty sure this is put on for my benefit, or at least played up, but I want to strangle him anyway.

Then he says, 'Listen, love, I can drive in here but it'll be two quid extra on the meter, or there's a drop-off car park just a couple of hundred yards this way, you can walk the extra distance and save yourself the cash.' Apparently it is a weird thing with the car parks in the airport.

'Thank you so much,' I say, and mean it.

Tiny bits of kindness. They can make all the difference.

When I get inside and go through security (no water bottles to throw out this time), the plane is delayed. I want to scream. Of course it is. Of course it fucking is. It's a fucking Irish plane and we are a nation of incompetent dicks.

'You again!' a voice calls as I stomp past one of the bars.

I turn around. Me? Does she mean me? And then I realise it's Black Dress.

'Hi,' I say, suddenly shy.

'We're on the same flight, are we?' She nods towards the

181

departures board. 'Late as usual.'

'Yeah.'

'Sit down,' she invites, patting the seat next to her.

'I'm –' I'm about to say I'm not old enough to legally drink, as in if anyone needs ID I'm screwed, but on the day that it is, I don't care.

'You're only a babby,' she guesses. 'It's grand. But can I get you a drink?'

We're not supposed to, for at least forty-eight hours after. Can make the bleeding worse. But mine hasn't started yet and if it does I will want hardcore pain relief. So.

'Go on so,' I say, sliding into the seat.

Her name's Rosemary and she's thirty-nine and she has two kids. 'Two's more than enough,' she says. 'I couldn't do it.'

Off my look she says, 'Ah here, don't be looking at me like that. It's hard work. I'd rather be a good mam to the two of them than a bad mam to three.'

'I wasn't being judgey or anything,' I hasten to reassure her. 'I just thought – like, earlier, looking around, I was so sure everyone had, you know, the *right* reasons. The worthy ones. You know what I mean?'

She nods. 'I know exactly what you mean.'

'What are your kids like?' I say suddenly.

Her face lights up. 'Gorgeous,' she says. 'I don't just mean on the outside, they're just gorgeous girls, the pair of them. Lovely kids. Kind, you know? Sarah's twelve, Amy's ten. They're minding a neighbour's dog for him at the moment, they're mad about animals.'

A drink and a half later and Rosemary wants to know why I'm getting weepy. 'Pet, are you all right? What's up? The hormones can play havoc with you, you know.'

I sniff. 'I just wish my mum talked about me the way you talk about your daughters.' *In vino veritas*. Talk about overshare. But it feels okay to tell Rosemary.

'I bet she does,' Rosemary says, but I am not convinced.

Our gate is finally announced, and she stands up, wincing a little. 'Starting, I think,' she says. 'I'm going to run to the loo, pet, you go ahead.' She wraps her arms around me tight. 'Mind yourself,' she whispers in my ear.

'You too,' I say.

On the plane, I'm at the window. Halfway through the flight, the middle-seat and aisle-seat grumble as I clamber over them to get to the bathroom, but, well, fuck them. I replace my pad – the world's largest, seriously – and pull my knees up to my chest for a few minutes, breathing through the pain. The wine earlier definitely helped. But the weird thing is how familiar it all is. Cramping uterus of doom and blood? Been there, done that.

And it's working, it's working, it's working, I don't need to ring them up in four weeks full of alarm, or go back, and even though I will still take that just-to-check test in a few weeks, I'm not afraid of it.

The nervous buzzing that's taken up residence in my chest and stomach and brain these past few weeks stills.

It's going to be okay.

I could float. I am pretty sure if they opened the doors to this plane, I'd glide my way home.

Home

Wake up in hell. Cram painkillers down my throat. Blood's soaked through my pyjama bottoms, but not – thank fuck – through the towel I put down.

And my mouth dry, my head throbbing. Alcohol. Drinks with Rosemary, who insisted on putting me in a taxi home after we landed in Dublin. I looked around for the others and couldn't find them. Maybe a different flight. Maybe White Hair and Dark Circles were staying overnight, staying up late watching movies like it was a sleepover.

Knock on my door. 'Lauren? You up?' Mum.

'I'll be out in a second!' I say, panicking. Can't let her see this much blood, even though it could just be a regular period for me. Did I see her when I got home? It was late. I don't remember. There is a gaping void in my memory.

'See you downstairs,' she says.

Quick shower, then into comfortable clothes – tracksuit bottoms and an old hoodie. Panic. It's back again. Does she know? There's not much she can do at this stage except lecture me, and lectures are nothing in comparison to your body not being your own.

In the kitchen, she's drinking a cup of coffee and looking through today's newspaper. 'You were stumbling around the place last night when you came in,' she says.

'Oh. I'm sorry.' Dark sinking feeling in my chest.

'I was going to get up to make sure you were all right, but by the time I did you were in bed asleep.'

Relief. I couldn't have said anything. She doesn't know.

'Honey,' she says, looking at me more tenderly than she has in months, 'you can't be coming home in a state like that. It's not safe for you, it's not good for your health . . .' She sighs, shakes her head. 'I'm not saying I want you to become a teetotaller, I *know* kids your age drink, and your dad and I have always let you have a glass of wine on special occasions. And I don't even mind if you're in Cork with your club and have a drink. *One.* Singular. All right?'

'All right,' I echo weakly.

'I mean,' she says, 'you don't find it hard to stop after just one, do you? Do we need to get you into counselling or anything?'

'Jesus, Mum, no. I'm sorry. We were drinking on the bus back and it got out of hand. It won't happen again. Promise.'

'Okay,' she says. She gives me a smile. 'Come here.'

And we have the kind of tender mother-daughter hug we used to have way more of before her new job, only it's about entirely the wrong thing.

The weird thing is, a few years ago, when I was about eleven, I really wanted Mum to send me to a counsellor. Jessica, one of my friends from primary school was going to one, and I was *fascinated*. It seemed so glamorous and important, like you were a character on telly.

It seemed like it was saying that everything bad or scary swirling around in your head, all the things niggling at you, were real problems that mattered. Jessica's parents had split up, so that was a real problem. I knew that even if I had a fight with Mum or Dad it wasn't something I could really tell Jessica about. At least they were both still at home instead of living in different houses and saying mean things about one another.

I got sad sometimes, not just about stuff in my own life but about people dying in other countries. I really, really hated getting my period; I screamed every time it arrived. And sometimes I wanted to kiss people I knew I wasn't supposed to, like Jessica. But that was all normal. No one was stepping in and saying, 'Lauren, we'd like you to talk to someone. We think you matter.'

'Mum,' I said once when we she picked me up from some after-school activity, 'do you think I should go to a counsellor?'

She laughed. 'Why do you want to go to see a counsellor, honey? What's up?'

It was hard to put it into words. It felt stupid. I just wanted someone, a grown up, to talk to. Someone who wasn't one of my parents. 'Nothing,' I said. 'I was just *wondering*.'

'I don't know where we got you from,' she mused.

'If you're not sure about that then we might need to have a talk about the birds and the bees, Mum.'

She cracked up, and eventually I joined in.

Watching

Online. Videos. A blond American woman sobbing hysterically about God not forgiving her for her abortion because she can't have any kids now. Another blonde talking about how she was in the clinic and then heard the Lord speak to her and she walked out of there and now her son is the greatest blessing of her life.

I feel like they're kinda crazy but I can't stop watching them. My laptop is warm across my abdomen, helping soothe the pain of the cramps. I let the videos keep playing. There are so many of them.

School

Have you ever tried 'walking like a boy' while dying of cramps? Have you? Because that's exactly what I'm doing on our second day back at school after Christmas. We are singing 'The Boy Friend' and marching around the place 'like men', wide stance.

I have seriously-bleeding-through fear and would rather keep my legs tight together, if you don't mind, Carmel. For a moment I imagine saying this. Going into an extraordinary amount of detail about it all. How very unladylike it is to talk about womanly things.

'Swing your arms a bit more! You're strutting!' Mrs O'Connor instructs.

I don't think I have ever taken up so much space in my life. I imagine what it would be like to live like this.

As soon as the bell rings, I race to the nearest bathroom. I deal with the blood and flush. Evan comes in as I'm washing my hands.

I stare for a second. I dare him to notice something different about me. To understand.

'What?' He scowls.

And that bubble of possibility is firmly popped. 'You're

such an asshole. And Justin is not my pretend boyfriend.' He's not my boyfriend at all, I realise, but that's not the point here.

Evan looks at me with the kind of dismissive expression I am used to seeing on the faces of the cool girls. 'Whatever you say.'

'Like, why are you even so obsessed with saying I'm a lesbian, anyway? The *one fucking time* I ever slept with a girl –' But I stop. I can't get the rest of that sentence out. My throat is too full. My eyes are spilling over.

I push past Evan, and go in search of another bathroom to hide in.

'Did you have a nice Christmas, everyone?' Ms Lynch asks, and she indulges us for a few minutes – who went away, who stayed at home, who had family over, any exciting presents – before getting on to what we're doing in her class this term.

When Ms Lynch teaches English to other years it's just English, but because this is Transition Year it's broken up into weird chunks like Communications and Media, and Literature and Culture. The next thing we have to do is a group project on An Important Issue and how it's represented in the media. 'This can include not just newspapers, magazines but also films, books, TV programmes, games . . . anything you think might be relevant.'

I end up in a group with Fee, Ann-Marie and Evan. Because the universe has a sense of humour. Or, more likely, Ms Lynch thinks Evan and I need to work together and become friends again.

'So,' Ann-Marie says brightly as we pull our chairs together, 'any suggestions for our topic?' Her hand is poised over a brand-new A4 pad, ready to jot down what we say in her annoyingly neat handwriting.

I have thoughts. I just don't want to share them with someone so . . . *irritating*.

'How about the environment?' Ann-Marie suggests, jotting that down. 'Or . . . exams.'

'Human trafficking,' I finally offer.

Ann-Marie purses her lips. 'I don't think that's really appropriate for *school*, Lauren.'

'Fine.' I cross my arms.

Fee follows suit, and Evan is too busy drawing on the cover of his homework journal to pay much attention to anything else. By the time Ms Lynch wanders over to us, we're sitting there sullenly.

'How're you getting on over here?' she asks.

'We're struggling with ideas,' Ann-Marie says in a way that indicates it's ever-so-tiresome for her to work with such useless individuals as us.

Ms Lynch scans the group. 'Okay. All of you. First thing that comes into your head, no matter how silly you think it is. Evan. Go.'

'Gender identity,' Evan says immediately.

'Felicity.'

'Ummm . . . mental health.'

'Lauren.'

'Abortion,' I say.

This is the point where someone says something. Sees it. Ms Lynch asks if she can have a word with me. Something clicks in Evan's brain. Fee puts a hand to her mouth to cover a gasp.

Instead Ms Lynch just continues, 'Ann-Marie.'

'Exam stress,' Ann-Marie repeats.

'Okay,' Ms Lynch says cheerfully. 'Well, let's see – can you combine any of those? Mental health and exam stress would seem to go hand-in-hand, wouldn't they?'

We all nod.

She says more and I'm not listening. I can't. How can she not see it? How is it that everyone else is wandering around not *noticing*?

I tune back in just in time to hear Evan say something about '. . . driven to suicide.'

Ann-Marie lets out a huffy sigh. 'We're not going to bring suicide into this.'

'You're the one who suggested exam stress,' Evan says.

'Yes, but I don't immediately go to the worst-case scenario,' she says, a little snootily. 'Just because you like to act all *dark* and *depressed* . . .'

'Hey,' Fee says.

Ann-Marie's face is flushed now, but she keeps going. 'No, Felicity, *someone* needs to say it. There's nothing wrong with being happy or being – *normal*. Being a sad weirdo doesn't make you better than us.'

'Oh, screw you,' Evan says.

'It's so hard being normal,' I say solemnly. 'Poor little Ann-Marie.'

'And you!' she shrieks. 'You're just as bad.'

Well, now, *that* I resent. My hand is out of my control before I realise it. My right palm slams its way across her left cheek.

'Lauren!' Ms Lynch yells. She is Not Happy.

While everyone else is still discussing their group project ideas, I am outside in the corridor with Ms Lynch doing the 'not angry just disappointed' face at me.

'Look, Lauren, that wasn't on.'

'She started it.'

'You're sixteen, not six. Cop the fuck on.'

Weirdly, the swearing is what makes me snap back into proper respect mode.

'Okay. Sorry.'

'I'm not the one you need to apologise to.'

'Yeah, but you're *easier* to apologise to.'

She tries to hide a smile. 'Come on. I know she can be difficult. It's no reason to get violent with her. Violence never solves anything.'

'I must have missed that part of history where World War Two was solved with a lovely cup of tea and a chat.'

'Lauren.'

'I'll say sorry to her.'

'And maybe at least *try* to make it sound sincere?'

'Can I try it from across the classroom while she's in another group?'

'No.' The corners of her mouth are twitching.

'All right.'

'Okay then.'

'Everything all right?' another voice calls from down the corridor. Of course it's her. Mrs O'Connor stops and says, 'What's going on here?'

'Just having a chat, Carmel,' Ms Lynch says breezily, offering up a fake smile.

Mrs O'Connor looks suspicious, but nevertheless moves on.

I look at Ms Lynch. Ms Lynch looks at me.

'Go on, get back in there,' she says, mock-wearily. And then, just as I am about to turn the handle, she adds, 'Lauren?'

'Yeah?'

'If that had happened when my back wasn't turned, I'd be filling out a report right about now. For your own sake – don't put me in that position again.'

I nod.

I should be grateful. It's just that she's being nice about the *wrong fucking thing*.

Message

I haven't read it since the summer, but now I find it again, scroll back up until I get to the date, a week after I walked home from Steph's house alone and confused and worried.

Seven days of silence and then this.

Laur, sorry for radio silence. Been thinking and need to tell you something. I'm a boy (at least inside – you know what I mean, you know how it all works). Not telling anyone else yet so please don't share but thought you should know. Sx

And it doesn't matter that it's been months, because the same rush of 'what the actual fuck?' hits me. A wave of so many things, from 'maybe I should have known this before we slept together' to 'exactly when did you decide this?' and all with a dark, unsettling cloud of 'this is not real and please stop it'.

My reply at the time, still there: *Thanks for telling me. Lx*

That was it, then. Photos started popping up of Steph and Marc hanging out together. I went to songwriting camp and got together with Justin. We came back to school to a new timetable that let us avoid each other. Still *friends*. Still talking to one another and 'liking' statuses posted online and seeing each other at Q Club. But not what we were.

Not even close.

And now. Now, nothing at all.

The Dublin Journal, 12 January

ANTI-CHOICE CLINIC MASQUERADING AS CRISIS PREGNANCY CENTRE

Having an abortion increases your risk of cancer, damages your mental health irrevocably, and makes you likely to abuse future children, a counsellor at an alleged crisis pregnancy centre claims.

Following an anonymous tip from a young Irish woman who visited the clinic seeking advice on travelling for an abortion, the Dublin Journal *sent a reporter undercover to investigate. Sharon Pollard presented herself as seven weeks pregnant and sought advice about her options from the Women's Advice Clinic on Marian Street in the city centre.*

'The girl who contacted us said she'd been told it was too late for her to have a medical abortion at seven weeks,' Pollard notes, 'and I wondered if the counsellors there would give the same advice to a thirty-year-old woman as they would a teenager. As it turned out, I had an almost identical experience.'

Pollard was advised that it was too late for a medical abortion – an option that is typically available to women who are up to nine weeks pregnant – and that surgery was the only option. 'The counsellor showed me a picture of a foetus in the womb and explained in graphic detail how surgery would "hurt the baby". I asked about the gestational age of the foetus and she fobbed me off, even though it was very clear the image was of a third-trimester foetus viable outside the womb, rather than an embryo.'

The clinic also informs women that their risk of breast cancer is increased by undergoing an abortion. 'There is absolutely no scientific basis for this claim,' Dr Thomas Foley of the National Maternity Institute says. Nor are there any reputable studies which link abortion to future child abuse or mental illness, although Foley notes that the strain of secrecy for women in countries where abortion is illegal or extremely limited can be stressful.

'The lack of regulation in Ireland around these agencies is appalling and a serious threat to women's health,' Dr Andrea O'Keeffe, chairperson of MPFC (Medical Professionals For Choice). 'Women facing unexpected pregnancies must be clearly informed of every option available to them, including their right to travel for a termination if they so choose.'

An ongoing list of rogue crisis pregnancy agencies in the state can be found here. Cliona Reilly of the Irish Pro-Choice Alliance adds, 'Many of these agencies move around frequently and reappear under different names. They also – as in the case of the Women's Advice Clinic – often situate themselves close to legitimate family planning centres in a further attempt to mislead vulnerable women.'

'So many of the women there didn't have English as their first language and probably didn't know that you ARE allowed to *travel for an abortion, even if it's illegal here,' our anonymous contact reported, a pattern Pollard also observed on her visit to the clinic. 'It's unbelievably horrible that they're allowed lie to them like that. To lie to us. How is this acceptable?'*

Email

I start shaking when I see it. The online edition, but I know we have a print copy of the paper in our sitting room.

There it is. What happened. My words. Backed up by a real journalist.

So weird to come home from a day of singing and dancing to see people linking to this.

I haven't checked my Irish Girl account since I sent the emails, but I log in now, see replies, including several emails from the *Dublin Journal* asking if they can get a phone number for me, and then finally one from last night letting me know that the story would run today.

I should feel proud or brave or something, but all I can think is: what if someone figures it out?

And then I think: what if no one does?

At dinner I wait for either of my parents to bring it up. We talk about the weather.

Nightclub

A special treat for a Friday: we watch Imelda and Ann-Marie, as Polly and Tony, run through their first scene together. Polly has ordered a fabulous costume to wear for the ball – but no one to go with! Gasp! All of her Perfect Young Lady friends have a date! What's a girl to do?

Fortunately, the boy delivering the outfit (Tony) is super-charming. Sure, he's only a delivery boy, and Polly is wealthy, but who cares when this is true love? All of this happens in about two minutes. It's sort of like when Anna and Hans fall in insta-love in *Frozen*, except there's no lovely gruff ice merchant to come along and point out the ridiculousness of love-at-first-sight.

'Oh, young love,' Tara says beside me, pretending to wipe away a tear.

'It's magical,' I deadpan right back.

The bell eventually goes for lunch. 'Shop?' Tara invites.

'Sure.'

'Oh my God,' she says as we're putting our coats on, 'did you see that story about the fake abortion clinic? Awful.'

'Yeah,' I say. 'I can't believe they let these places . . .'

This is so surreal. Still bleeding, lighter now but *still*, and we're talking about me.

'I know. It's *horrible*.' Tara looks on the verge of tears. 'Can you imagine, like?'

Yes.

I don't know why I can't say it. I don't know why the words won't come out now.

'Fair play to the woman who tipped them off, though,' Tara says. 'I mean, at least now people know, and it'll get shut down . . .'

Maybe that's it. Maybe it will get shut down. And from the outside, that's a happy ending. A victory for the good guys.

But it doesn't change anything for the women who have been there already. It doesn't change a damn thing.

'D'you want to go out tonight?' I ask Tara when she's run out of steam. 'Get our minds off the crapness of this country?'

'Yeah, sure,' she says immediately. 'Will we ask Fee?'

'Yeah. And if there's anyone else you want to come along . . .'

She looks like she's about to say something, but then doesn't. 'This'll be fun,' she says instead. Full of optimism. I look at her with wonder.

We get groped in the nightclub – not technically an underage venue but everyone here looks about the same age as us and is drinking – and decide to tell everyone that we're lesbians in the hope of deflecting male attention. (Does it work? Of course it doesn't. The only safe way to get guys in places like these to leave you alone is to tell them you have a boyfriend, and even that doesn't always work.)

'I *should* be a lesbian,' Tara decides at one point.

'I don't think it works that way,' Fee says kindly.

'No harm in trying it out, though,' I add. 'Just in case. You never know! Live wildly! Seize the –'

My inspirational quoting is interrupted by Tara flinging her face towards mine and offering up a very enthusiastic snog. I go for it, because I am only human, and then she lurches back and decides it is now time to be sick.

Shockingly, we get thrown out.

'Let's go back to mine,' Fee offers, which I am relieved by, because I can't go home yet if I've been drinking; I do not need the parentals sniffing my breath and assessing my ability to walk in a straight line. (I've never felt that I *wasn't* able to walk in a straight line but maybe you don't notice, if you're that drunk?) And this way we don't have to hand Tara over to her family while she's still a bit wobbly.

'Love being out with my girls,' Tara says sleepily as we get on the bus, and even though it's totally the booze talking, I feel it too. Me and Fee grin at each other, and Tara rests her head on my shoulder.

Enter Ellie and Sandra. This is how I think it, like we're all on stage – really should've gotten a part in the musical – except how it actually happens is they get on the bus at the next stop after us, and Ellie looks at me and then looks away, but Sandra says 'hey' to Tara and it turns out they know each other, so before we know it all five of us are back in Fee's house. And I'm wondering where the Satanist brother is and she reminds me that's Tara, and then we are making drinks and listening carefully for a car pulling up outside, because Fee's parents are out to dinner.

'They'll be out late,' she says. 'It's some corporate thing, but just in case . . . like, they don't mind me having friends over, but, y'know.'

She is a little bit fuzzy around the edges. Or maybe I am.

Ellie and Sandra are being very clearly not-just-friends, which I guess makes sense – it's not like there's any other reason for just the two of them to hang out together – but it feels weird to watch them snuggling and know that Sandra also hangs out with Justin's friends and is/was maybe a girlfriend of one of them.

(I really hope she doesn't have a boyfriend and isn't just messing around with Ellie on the side. Having her cake and eating it too. Okay, that's a stupid phrase, obviously you're going to eat your cake, but you're only supposed to take one slice. Or if you're taking two slices you should at least tell the – um – baker. My metaphors may be derailing but there's something up here and I am anxious.)

Or maybe I'm just jealous, watching them all cuddly and couple-ish together. That urge hits: I want a *person*.

I take out my phone and start a text to Justin, and Ellie looks over and has this very obvious Dilemma Face before finally standing up and saying, 'You sure you want to drunk-message, Laur?'

'I'm not drunk,' I say. I am *drinking*. There is a difference.

'Who is it? Your boy? Is he still your boy?'

'None of your business.'

Ellie sighs. 'Come on, don't be an idiot, give me your phone.'

'Nope. You hate me.' And suddenly I'm tearful.

203

'I don't – oh, Jesus, Lauren, you said some really shitty things. You can't go around saying trans girls aren't real girls, like.'

Properly crying now. I can't believe how easily the tears come. Might be the gin. 'I know. I didn't want to hurt you, I just – I don't think you get how, how, scary, how . . .' I'm hyperventilating.

Ellie sighs, goes in for the back-rub again. 'Come on. Breathe.'

My hands swat her away. 'I don't want you being nice to me if you hate me,' I wail.

'I don't hate you,' she sighs. 'But I have to say something if you're out of line, Laur, you get that, right?'

I can't make words any more. I cry and cry and Ellie's on one side of me and Tara's on the other and they both look terrified.

'Babe, come on, what's up?' Ellie says, stroking my hair. 'Is it Evan?'

I gesture towards Tara. 'Show Ellie the story,' I whisper.

Tara pulls it up on her phone, getting all weepy herself (gin is not a good drink for her, I realise). By the time Ellie's finished reading it, she looks properly horrified. 'Fucking hell. They need to burn that place to the ground.'

I nod. Tearfully.

And then of all people, it's Sandra who says, from her space leaning against the radiator, 'Can we just accept that everyone in this room is screwed over in some way and get on with the drinking?'

'Hear hear!' Tara says.

'That work for you?' Ellie asks, tilting my chin up to look at her. Like a mother might. (She could have been my person in Liverpool, I think. My eyes fill up again.)

'Yeah,' I say, putting on a brave face.

She pulls me in for a hug. Whispers, 'Some advice from someone who's been through fuckloads of therapy . . . you have to talk to someone. Okay?'

I nod into her shoulder, even though I don't mean it. Because then we're all laughing and chatting and it's all safe and okay. Or maybe that's the booze. Because when I wake up on the floor of Fee's bedroom the next morning I still feel scared. Of what, I don't know. But scared. All the way through me.

Morning

Sent messages:

I really need to talk to you about something.

Justin this is important seriously.

Youre such a fuckwit omg cant believe i ever slept with you

Do you even know what importantant means omg

You are duck a dick

Fasd YUfsdfd Gad d

Helksd jersa rrraasssds

Asfnjfasutre fdsjjf sock

Amazingly, he has not replied.

And, okay, I know the later messages verge into obvious-crazy-drunk-girl territory, but isn't he wondering at all? Doesn't he even care?

How is it that I'm still seeping blood and scared of anyone finding out and he's just – getting on with his life?

Choose Life press statement, 14 January

CHOOSE LIFE STATEMENT ON ROGUE CRISIS PREGNANCY AGENCIES

Deirdre O'Connor, vice-chair of Choose Life, has condemned the Women's Advice Clinic for misleading vulnerable pregnant women, as reported in the *Dublin Journal* and others this week.

'It is vital that women facing an unplanned pregnancy are given accurate information,' she states. 'However, we must also ensure that the pro-life message is not censored by the liberal media. Many women experience deep regret following a termination, feeling pressured to choose an easy solution without fully considering its long-term effects. We frequently hear from women who have been traumatised by their experience of abortion. We must resist the pro-abortion agenda and ensure that the life of the unborn child in this country is protected.'

Radio

On Sunday morning the radio is on in the kitchen. Deirdre O'Connor is on one of those talk shows representing 'one side' of 'the abortion debate', going on about her own daughter who's sixteen and needs to be protected from the dangerous 'pro-abortionists', and I realise this is Imelda's mother. Carmel's sister or sister-in-law.

She keeps talking over the medical doctor who's on with her. Keeps saying 'the life of the unborn child'.

Dad comes in as I am violently buttering my toast. It takes him a few seconds to actually listen to what's on the radio, and as soon as he does he rolls his eyes and goes, 'She's a headcase, that one.'

'Yeah,' I say.

Say *more*, Dad. Say how horrible it must be to have an unwanted pregnancy in this country. Say how sympathetic you are. I need you to spell it out for me. Say how if it was me who'd gone to a clinic like that, who'd been lied to like that, you'd be raging. You wouldn't judge me. You'd still love me. *Say it*.

'Any plans for today?' he asks.

I shrug. 'Not really.'

Photos

I stare at the photos they've uploaded from over the last few weeks. The 'lads'. Justin, Cassidy, Murphy, Kelly, a few others. Various poses, looking so cool, so macho.

The Justin in these photos – the one ignoring my admittedly crazy-drunk messages – is a stranger. He is a boy, a stupid careless boy who doesn't ever have to think about the consequences of his actions. No one is on the radio debating whether or not he should have to travel to England for a medical procedure. No one's judging him.

I think about the sex. That week of really incredible sex we had. But I'm still cramping and feeling gross and it doesn't get me as excited as it once might have.

(I think about fingers sliding up inside me. Eyes locked onto mine.)

Status update: *Penises are gross. Totally becoming a lesbian.* I tag Tara and Fee in this. And then, with more than a hint of grumpiness, Justin.

The first reply is, weirdly, from Murphy: *pity!!! ;)*

Justin's response is to un-tag himself and then delete me from his friends list. There's no broken-heart image that pops

209

up on the screen for this kind of thing, but somehow that just makes it worse.

And that's when I decide what I'm going to do.

An Exercise in Online Small Talk:

    Me: *Hey you, how's it going?*

    Murphy: *Not too bad, how about you?*

    Me: *4th year, can't complain! ;)*

    Murphy: *Ah yeah forgot you were only a baby!! We've loads of work in 5th year.*

    Me: *You poor thing.*

    Murphy: *It's okay, we got our doss year last year.*

    Murphy: *You doing anything cool for TY?*

    Me: *Musical! It's dire!*

    Murphy: *Ah no!*

    Me: *Yeah! So cringy.*

    Murphy: *You have a big part in it?*

    Me: *Nope, nothing!*

    Murphy: *Pity, you're a really good singer.*

    Me: *Aw, thank you. <3*

    Murphy: *;)*

This is a beginning.

Costumes

By the second-last week in January our costumes are almost ready for the musical and we try them on for a rehearsal. Cream trousers and matching jumpers for the 'gentlemen', our hair pulled back in plaits and tucked beneath our shirt collars. I feel lumpy and gross. I want to be dressed in something elaborate like Fee is, as the overdressed headmistress, or something dainty like Tara. Tara has loads of different costumes – a pretty dress for the first act, a striped swimsuit for the second, a clown outfit for the third – and she looks fabulous in all of them.

Today we're doing a number that Tara has with a bunch of the 'boys' – it starts off with those cross-dressing girls who actually have speaking parts and then we, the chorus, come along halfway through. When this thing finally goes on stage I'll be waiting backstage for any song I'm in. That's what we do. It's called 'Safety in Numbers' and it's basically about how Tara's character, Maisie, is flirting with all these different guys and keeping them dangling. It's already very clear that she's going to end up with Bobby, who she has a duet with in the first act, but as the plot is pretty flimsy, we have this number.

March, march, march. We do a lot of walking heavily and

letting girls – the girls-playing-girls, I mean – twirl around us. I watch as the girls-playing-boys lift Tara up into the air and hold her there.

Maybe I didn't get to be Maisie because I weigh more than a feather. Instead of talent this is about who's least likely to cause a disaster by thudding onto the ground. I am as tall as any of the girls playing the macho men.

My plait is itching to be unleashed, and I want to take off this heavy jumper so the world can see I have breasts. I am woman, hear me roar. I can't pretend. I can't pretend to be anything other than this fleshy cage with breasts and a womb and a vagina and everything that goes with that.

And oh, don't think I don't know how much easier it would be if I really was the boy I'm pretending to be, that uncomplicated default human. Not needing to think and worry about my body in the same way. Not having bits of my body be the subject of national debate.

I see what's happening like I'm floating above it. In this show, the girls are tiny and delicate and they skip and twirl and do proper dancing. The boys stomp around the stage. The ones with names will get to propose at the end, and everyone will be nicely married off. It's a parody that doesn't even feel like one because we want the world to be like this. And because it is a shitty excuse for a musical and it says nothing important and I want something *more*.

But maybe I wouldn't think this if it were me and not Tara skipping around the place like a mischievous fairy, destined to be the star of the show.

Game

Q Club have arranged an 'outing' (yes, everyone is sniggering at the choice of words) for Saturday to some subtitled movie about being gay in some country I probably should know where it is but feel too tired to care about.

Evan puts up a self-righteous status giving facts and figures about gay rights around the world and if I hadn't planned on skipping it that'd definitely have made me.

So when Ellie messages specifically to ask me if I'm going (and if I'm okay after being all weepy that night), I lie and say I have to go see family. I repeat the same story to Fee and Tara when they're planning a movie night in, and then I tell my parents I'm not feeling well, and I retreat to my bedroom for the evening with a bottle of vodka and a carton of orange juice – vitamin C! Healthy!

I don't need to get up early in the morning and go to school. I don't need to get out of anyone's house at a reasonable hour. I don't need to do anything until Monday morning, far away, and it gets further with every sip.

Just me and my phone and my laptop and my drink and that's all I need. To follow up on the late-night messages of the last couple of weeks.

Easier to send sexy messages when drinking. Murphy has so far not sent me a dick pic but earlier this week I did allude to having received one in the past so it may well be on the way. Sometimes I feel like he's borrowed some handbook for How To Sext, because he keeps going on about my 'tits' and how much he'd like to 'cum' on them, and – really, dude: not sexy.

But it's a game, all a game. I see that now. So I type back nonsense, the kind he seems to expect. *Oh baby, yeah. You're so sexy. Getting wet just thinking about you.*

I'm actually drinking and watching comedies on Netflix but I type nonsense about doing things to myself, blah blah blah, what does it even matter? At some point in the evening, moving onto some beer hidden behind old school reports in my wardrobe, I have an epiphany. Gender is not nuanced. It really is completely fucking binary. Women are copped-on and men are morons like Murphy who just think about sex all the time and will say or do whatever they think it takes to get it. That is how the world works. We are nothing but our biology. Men are completely and utterly ruled by their dicks.

And completely on cue, another message arrives from Murphy and yes, it is indeed that aubergine-shaped thing that is utterly unattractive out of context.

So hot, I message back. And then, for ego-boosting, *And so big!!!*

He sends back a grinning face.

I take another gulp of beer.

Daily News (UK), 27 January

IRISH PRIME MINISTER DODGES
THE ABORTION QUESTION

The Taoiseach, Ireland's prime minister, has ignored demands from pro-choice groups that a referendum be held to repeal the eighth amendment of the Irish Constitution.

The amendment in question holds that the right of the unborn and the right of its mother are equal under Irish law. First put in place in 1983, the amendment has come under heavy criticism in recent years from the pro-choice lobby, particularly following a number of high-profile cases in which pregnant women's health and sometimes, tragically, lives, were put at risk. Most recently, an investigation into a rogue crisis pregnancy agency has returned the focus to the question of Irish women and their reproductive rights.

Deirdre O'Connor, a spokesperson for pro-life institute Choose Life, says, 'I commend the Taoiseach for not making any hasty decisions on this most serious matter. We should be proud of a constitution that protects the rights of all its citizens, including the unborn.'

Last year 3,571 women and girls accessing abortion services in the UK gave Irish addresses. The British Pregnancy Crisis Service note that many others give false addresses for confidentiality reasons, while those who cannot afford to travel often access the abortion pill online.

Thesis

Many new notifications when I wake up, fuzzy-headed. Many. Oh.

I hadn't realised I'd actually typed up my revolutionary thesis about gender and the driven-by-sex-ness of men and shared it with the universe (okay, not the entire universe, just my curated online-universe).

Basically we are all ruled by biology. The dudes want the sex because they think with their dicks and that's it, and the ladies spend so much time dealing with this that we don't actually have much energy left to think about what WE actually want. But suffice it to say we are not winning this.

Several paragraphs of earnestness from Evan about why this is problematic and incredibly transphobic, and then – oh – replies from me I don't even remember typing, eventually dissolving into name-calling.

Comment from Fee: *You're so hard on the poor men!! x*

Comment from John: *There is more to me than my dick.*

Second comment from John: *There are also my balls.*

I am about to reply with a laughing-face emoji when I realise I have done that already. Or rather, Past-Lauren has. Drunk Lauren.

A swooping dread overcomes me and then I remember: no one else is taking this that seriously. No one except Evan, and Evan is taking everything seriously these days. Everything except this friendship that we used to have.

So. So it's all fine. It's all okay. Everything's okay.

And then Ellie's private message comes in.

Darling, don't know & don't care at this stage if this is about Evan or something else but you need to stop posting this shit & (don't hate me) were you drunk last night? Please go talk to a counsellor or someone. Worried about you. xxx

Worried about me but still basically on Evan's side. I get it. I thought we were okay. I thought maybe she understood. I thought she might even have fucking figured it out. But no.

Nice work on ruining another one of my friendships, I message Evan. *Get someone else to do your dirty work next time.*

Evan: *WTF?*

Lauren: *You know exactly what I mean.*

Evan: *??? No. What?*

Evan: *And any time you want to apologise is fine . . .*

Evan: *No?*

Lauren: *You ever going to apologise to me?*

Evan: *You're the one in the wrong here.*

Lauren: *HOW THE FUCK CAN YOU BE SO CLUELESS?*

Lauren: *We are done. We are so done.*

Evan: *Yeah, too fucking right. Have a nice life.*

Deleting

There is a beautiful freedom in just cutting people out of your life. So much easier to do online than in person, of course. Remove Ellie. Remove Evan. Definitely remove Marc. Remove myself from any group chats where I might have to interact with any of them, hear anything about them.

There is a little heartbreak in wondering if anyone will notice, or comment. If John, say, might get in touch and ask how I'm doing, what's up. Heartbreak because of course no one does, or if they do, they're not saying anything.

IRISH PRIME MINISTER DODGES THE ABORTION QUESTION and they don't even care.

(I don't need them. Any of them. I don't need anyone from Q Club any more.)

Perfect

The chorus declare themselves Perfect Young Ladies through song, delivering the lines without a trace of irony. This is the first musical number in the show, and I know from YouTube clips that there's supposed to be something tongue-in-cheek about it.

The trouble is, when you have (mostly) girls who aspire to some imagined perfect ideal of womanhood playing Perfect Young Ladies, it doesn't quite work. These are the dream, gathered together on one side of the assembly hall: beautiful slender figures, no one over five foot four. All of them – even Evan with a boyish haircut – look the part.

I am not a Perfect Young Lady in the musical or in real life. As the rehearsal crawls along, I let my mind drift to unladylike things. Murphy thrusting inside me. Heavy on top of me. Grunting with pleasure.

After it's finished we will lie back on the pillows and light cigarettes, even though the one time I tried to smoke I ended up looking an absolute fool, and then I will say something apt and cutting. Like, *You're better than Maguire.*

And he'll grin and act like of course he is. Later he'll tell all his friends about what's happened, and I will be the sexy girl they all want and they will think Justin is an idiot for abandoning me.

I will be the dream-girl that doesn't really exist but he'll regret me. He will rue the day. He'll turn up at my house begging for me to take him back and I'll roll my eyes and tell him grandly, *Go home, Justin*.

'What're you smirking about?' Fee wants to know, nudging me. She's on a break from her special rehearsal, hanging out with us lowly humans.

'Oh, nothing,' I say, feeling my face heat up.

'Hmmm,' she says, sceptically.

We have agreed on a time and place. Tonight (Friday), his house – but I need to be out of there by eleven because his parents will be back from the theatre. I asked what they're going to see and he doesn't have a clue.

(He is such a boy. But isn't that the point? They're all like this. Just want the sex. That's fine. That's all I want to do. Not for the sex itself. For the having it. For being wanted in that way.)

The intercom crackles. The secretary's voice. 'Can Lauren Carroll please come to the principal's office? Lauren Carroll to the office, please.'

Mother

I ignore the 'oooh, you're in trouble'-type calls from various morons in the class and trudge down the corridor.

Why couldn't she have just texted me? (Okay, we're not supposed to have our phones on in school, except everyone does and she knows it.)

I knock on the outside door – the secretary's – who then calls Mum on the phone to say 'Lauren's here' rather than just tap on the inner door.

'You can go in now,' the secretary says, like she's doing me a favour.

Mum's behind her desk. 'Lauren,' she says. 'Sit.'

I sit, and then hate myself for doing it. She's in principal-mode now, not mother-mode, and I can't think of anything recent I could be in trouble for, so why am I acting like an obedient lapdog?

'I got my credit card statement yesterday.'

Shit.

'There's a return flight on it to Liverpool.'

'That's weird,' I say.

'I asked your dad and he doesn't know anything about it.

And I rang the airline in case the card had been stolen but then they told me the flight was for . . .' She waits for me to fill in the gap.

I say nothing.

'When was it for?' she prompts.

I shrug.

Her mouth tightens. 'The day you were supposed to be in Cork.'

I stare at her. This isn't fair. Mum stuff in school is not fair.

'Come on, say something,' she says impatiently.

'I'll pay you back when I can,' I say finally.

She lets out a heavy breath and props her chin up with her right hand. 'Who did you go with? It wasn't Stephanie, was it? I don't want to have to tell Geraldine . . .'

'No one,' I say.

She sighs again. 'Lauren. I'm not an idiot. I know why Irish women go to Liverpool for the day.'

Here it is. The moment. Yes, she's been caught up with her new job. Yes, she's been too busy to notice the rise and fall of her daughter's relationship. But now. Now she sees.

And then she says it. 'I never thought I'd say this, but thank God you're not . . . well, you know. Was it Stephanie or was it another friend of yours?'

I feel dizzy, like this is happening to someone else. 'Another friend,' I manage.

She nods. Offers up a tight little smile. 'I'm glad she had you with her.' And then she tells me the story of going over to London with Auntie Maeve twenty years ago, just after she'd met Uncle Gerry. 'They were going to get married but they were still years off wanting kids,' she says.

'But they had kids,' I say, confused, listening to family history reshape itself as Mum keeps talking.

'Later,' she says. Sonya, who's twelve now. Jason, eight.

'Anyway,' Mum continues, 'we'll call it even on the credit card charge, all right? But if anything like this ever happens again – look, honey, we need to know where you are, okay? What if something happened?'

(Something *did* happen.)

I nod. My throat is too thick with tears to say anything.

On my way to my locker to get my lunch, I feel the impending collapse and dart into the nearest bathroom before sinking to the floor. Like they do on TV, I think vaguely, as the crumpled-up hysterical sobbing begins.

For some reason I keep thinking about the summer when I was twelve-turning-thirteen and me and Mum binge-watched all of *Gilmore Girls* on Netflix, the ultimate mother-daughter show, and how it felt – with Dad at work all day and Brian recently emigrated – like it was just the two of us in the family, like we too could have quirky, speedy repartee and in-jokes and a special bond.

But, you know. TV lies.

Run

'TV lies, basically,' I say to Fee that afternoon. We're in the library for English class today, finishing up our group projects.

'I've heard that,' she says.

'Shhh,' Ann-Marie hisses from across the table.

I glare at her. She's been insufferable ever since I had to apologise to her. I mean, more insufferable. 'We're allowed to talk, Ann-Marie, it's a group project.'

She lets out a huffy sigh but doesn't respond.

'Right,' Fee says, 'which ones are we putting in?'

Ms Lynch made us all narrow down our topics once we had a general theme, so our group is looking at the representation of school-leaving exam stress in popular media. Fee and I have watched a lot of clips from American teen dramas about taking the SATs or having meltdowns before finals, and read lots of Buzzfeed articles with titles like 'Nine completely unrealistic moments in *Gossip Girl*'.

I shrug. 'I don't care.'

'Sounds about right,' Evan says from across the table.

Fee looks startled. 'What?'

'Lauren doesn't care about anyone but herself.' This is said as cool, dispassionate fact.

'Look who's talking,' I spit out even as Fee says, 'That's not fair.'

Ann-Marie looks amused. 'Have our resident lesbian couple broken up?'

'Shhh,' I hiss back.

Fee tugs on my arm, and we scoot our chairs a bit away from the table. 'You okay? What did your mum want to talk to you about?'

'Nothing. Just home stuff.'

'That must be really weird.'

'Yep,' I say tightly.

'D'you wanna talk about it?'

'Nope.'

'You sure?'

'I SAID NO!' My voice is louder than I meant it to be. My hands are trembling. Everyone in the library has turned around to look at me.

'Lauren, are you –' Ms Lynch starts.

Am I what? Am I okay? AM I FUCKING OKAY?

No one really wants to know the answer to that. They can't fix this. No one can fix this.

(Curling my legs up to my chest in a tiny airplane bathroom and breathing through the pain instead of being at home in my own bed.)

(Brian's money.)

(Mum's credit card.)

(Lying to Dad about a trip to Cork and pocketing cash.)

(Every single bit of my savings that I was going to use to buy clothes or books or sweets or the kind of things normal teenage girls buy, gone.)

(My words in the news and still nothing changes.)

(Both sides of the debate. Like there are sides.)

. . . we see a lot of abuse with these women . . .

Maybe you do, crazy fake counsellor, because I want to hit and scream and scrape and tear and how could anyone trust me with anyone ever?

This is my body, which will be given up for you.

'Lauren,' Ms Lynch says again. Her hand on my arm. I fling it off.

She looks scared. So does Fee. They should be. I'm scared. I run.

Swarm

The rain means I opt for the bus rather than walking, but I regret this as soon as I realise that the fifth- and sixth-years from Justin's school, who have a free last class on Fridays, are clustered at one of the bus stops. I sink down in my seat, hide my nose in a book.

They are a swarming mass, loud and laughing. I don't turn around to look at them, to see if I can spot anyone I know. They scare me, even though they're not doing anything to me. It's just that potential threat. Lurking. Lurking always.

Did I see it this much before? It's not like I've ever been properly assaulted. Unwanted gropes and kisses in nightclubs, the everyday kind of stuff. But now I am painfully aware of how vulnerable I am.

Any one of them could push me to the ground and rape me while the others cheered him on. Because they don't understand. They genuinely don't understand, they can't understand, what it means to live in this body. This body with its space to let men in. This body with its space to grow a new life, whether you want it or not. This body that has things done to it.

I can't do this any more. I can't live in this world.

Behind me, maybe two or three rows back, two lads chatting: 'I'd say she's more trouble than she's worth.'

'Ah, you'd be surprised. She's *filthy.*'

'Seriously?'

'Seriously, like.'

'Wouldn't have thought now. She's a bit dykey, isn't she?'

'Ha, wait till I show you.'

'Oh Jesus. No wonder Maguire put up with her. But she *is* fuckin' crazy.'

'She's mental, yeah, he said that. But . . .'

'Sure get the ride off her anyway.'

'Exactly.' Dirty laugh.

There is cold ice in my belly. I can't move.

She's mental, yeah, he said that.

'What're you doing, you perverts? Let me see!' another guy chimes in.

'Murphy's going after Maguire's ex,' the guy who must be Cassidy explains.

I can hear from the shuffling and movement that his phone's being passed around.

'She's a filthy bitch, isn't she?' someone says.

More laughter.

It could be worse, I remind myself. I could have sent a picture. Then a flash of panic: there's no chance I did, is there? Late at night with a drink in hand when things start dissolving? I root out my phone and go into the photos section, anxiously scrolling through. Nothing incriminating.

But there he is, sharing the stuff that I thought was

private – and they don't know and couldn't possibly understand that I was playing a game, a stupid game. They will think I really am that sexy up-for-it girl that Murphy wants, that he's half-directed in this particular role, and they'll judge me for it.

'Whore,' someone says.

'Slut,' someone else says.

There are other words too, other conversations going on, but these are the ones that pierce like arrows.

'Where *is* Maguire, anyway?' someone asks.

'Off sick.'

I'm relieved and then I wonder why. Would he have even cared that his ex-girlfriend is being called all these names, or would he just agree with them all? *Dirty whore slut bitch murderer.*

(No one's saying that last one, Lauren.)

(Why not? Why not add that to the pile?)

I stay on the bus longer than I need to. There is no way I'm turning around and letting them see my face. I stay on until the terminus, until everyone else has got off, and then I cross the road and wait for a bus back.

Take out phone again. Check bus app – one due in seven minutes, but I'll believe it when I see it. Then message Murphy. *Sorry, can't come over tonight, your dick's too tiny (like your brain!)!*

It doesn't make me feel better. I don't know what will.

Except that's a lie. I do know what will.

As soon as I'm home I change out of my uniform, put on some make-up, put on clothes that make me look older than I am but not trying too hard, and empty out a spare-change jar in the kitchen.

(I'm not an idiot. I will go to the supermarket with the automated check-outs where they will impatiently put in the code to let me buy booze and then be gone by the time I pour in coin after coin.)

(Or I will put it on my debit card and later deposit the coins in the bank to cancel out whatever is overdrawn.)

(Or I will . . . I don't know.)

Just to be safe I take a bottle of wine from the remainder of the Christmas stash and then pour some vodka into a water bottle and mix with Coke.

(Is this a good idea, Lauren?)

. . . she's mental, yeah, he said that . . .

. . . she was being real aggressive, like . . .

Was it Stephanie or was it another friend of yours?

Isn't this what normal teenage girls do? Drink and go out and flirt and not let any of this shit get to them? Isn't that so much easier?

I close the door behind me.

Strange

Wake up. Strange bed. Strange bedroom.

Boy's room. I think. Football posters. Games console hooked up to a screen. Handful of books, mostly thick fantasy volumes.

Head hurting. Mouth dry. Stomach – stomach fine until I sit up, and then turning somersaults. Heart beating too fast.

Wearing nothing. Naked. Clothes – where are clothes?

I step out of bed, find bra and knickers in opposite corners of the room. Then top and skirt and shoes and no tights but I don't care, I can live without them. My handbag. Fuck. Where's my bag?

Heart going faster and faster until I see a handle sticking out from under the bed. I fall on my bag like a lost child. Wallet – wallet there. Heavy with coins, no notes. Keys, yes. Phone – phone is there. Powered down but there. I look around for a charger, and find a trailing wire – yes. Here we go. I switch it on, watch the tiny battery on the screen fill and refill and urge it to go faster.

Whose room is this? Where am I? Where is the mysterious boy?

Please not Murphy. Yesterday on the bus floods back into my brain. No. I wouldn't have. I couldn't have.

(If it is not in my memory banks then it didn't happen. Nothing happened.)

Sometime last night I texted Dad to say I was staying at a friend's house. Message from Mum later asking was I okay. Oh. Ms Lynch's class. Right. Another flood of memory. I did not reply.

No other sent messages from me. Thank fuck. I go into photos, just to check. Photos of me and a boy. I am not looking straight at the camera. It seems I can't.

It's just a picture of us on the street, black night behind us, streetlights somewhere off to the right. Nothing dodgy. Nothing scary.

Except I have no idea who this boy is. And it looks like there's nothing behind my eyes. Just a vast empty space where my brain should be. Who is this girl in the picture? What has she let happen to her?

While the phone's still charging I check Google Maps. I am on the other side of the city from where I live.

Once I figure out where the nearest bus stop is to this place, I detach my phone and step outside, closing the door gently behind me. A house that looks like any other house except I have no idea whose it is. I tip-toe down the stairs.

Voices in the kitchen. I freeze. Then keep tip-toeing. The front door. A key in it, on the inside – I sag with relief. As soon as I reach it I turn the key and open the door, pulling it towards me. I slip out and tug it back into place, letting it click shut as quietly as I can.

Then I get the hell out of there.

***

233

Take no chances. In town, where I am anonymous, I go to a pharmacy and wait behind an old lady asking about something to do with swollen ankles before a friendly guy says, 'How can I help you?'

Had to be a guy.

'I'd like the morning-after pill,' I say.

He gets this look on his face and I'm scared he won't give it to me. He'll say that I shouldn't need it, that I shouldn't be having sex, that I should be safe – and I want to scream and say I am safe, at least I used to be . . .

(How did I get here?)

'All right, can you take a seat in there?' he says, indicating a white door marked 'Consultation Room'.

I push the door open. I take a seat.

Adrenaline hits and I am so, so tired. I am shredded. I could be packaging for a parcel, the stuff that spills out all over the floor when you rip open the thick brown paper and clogs up the vacuum cleaner.

I am not a girl any more. Not a person. I am a thing waiting in a tiny room. I am tired of waiting in rooms but it would take too much energy right now to move my arms and legs and propel myself out of this chair and out into the bustling Saturday-morning shopping crowd.

A woman comes in. Not the guy. I suppose this is deliberate. She's holding leaflets and a clipboard. 'You're looking for the morning-after pill?' she says.

I nod.

'Have you ever taken it before?'

I shake my head.

'Okay, so here's how it works . . .' she says, and I fade in and out. Stopping ovulation. Ninety-five percent effective if used within twenty-four hours.

'It's within twenty-four hours,' I say, wondering if I should admit that I don't even know if *it* is anything. Girls are always supposed to be able to tell but I can't. Whatever mystical connection I am supposed to have with my body has been severed.

(I'm being punished.)

(I don't even believe in God.)

(But it doesn't have to be God. Maybe just the universe. Maybe just my own body rebelling against me. This is what women's bodies do, isn't it?)

'And you know this should really be a last resort,' she says. 'You should be using a regular method of contraception, and if your partner hasn't recently been tested for STDs you should be using condoms.'

I know all this but she's treating me like I'm stupid and young and I can't find the words to object.

I nod and let her give me leaflets about different kinds of contraception. 'Remember, you still need to be protecting yourself against diseases even if you're on the Pill,' she says. 'I don't care how nice the guys are or what kind of families they come from. That doesn't tell you anything, understand?'

I *know* all this.

I nod. I am voiceless.

She eventually hands over the pill, a tiny sliver of a tablet attached to an unnecessarily large piece of cardboard, and gives me a glass of water to swallow it here and now. More instructions: if you get sick you need to come back. If your period doesn't arrive, you need to take a pregnancy test. (I don't say, 'Good job I still have a spare.')

Why am I getting lectured for doing the right thing? Isn't this what you're supposed to do, if there's a risk?

Is there *anything* you can do without being bad and wrong apart from hole yourself up in your bedroom and stay there forever?

Numb

More lectures at home. More being told about what I should be doing and how I shouldn't be losing my temper in school or staying over at friends' houses without giving parents more of a heads-up or ignoring text messages if they don't suit me.

Once upon a time I would have been sad or hurt or ashamed of all this and now . . . now I can't feel anything much.

I can't do anything right. This is my life now. I have no friends. No person. I am just a tiny girl-human in a vast, uncaring universe. Or if it does care, it doesn't approve of me.

I borrow some beers from Dad's collection. I go and watch the videos again.

If I'd known, I wouldn't have gone through with it . . . I felt powerless and kept asking myself 'what have you done?' . . . it changed me forever . . . I couldn't forgive myself until I found the Lord Jesus Christ . . .

The beer helps. The beer makes me able to cry. To feel sad. It's all so sad. It's all so very sad.

There is no quick fix for regret . . . I wish someone had told me . . . No one told me how guilty I would feel afterwards . . . I hated myself . . . I was in denial . . . when I gave birth to my next

child I was so afraid God would punish them because of what
I'd done . . .

The tears mean that I am a good person, deep down. That I feel bad about it. That I am having the right feelings, the appropriate feelings for a woman In This Situation.

I forgot to lock my door.

Mum is standing over me. My laptop, screen now black, lies askew on top of my duvet. Beer bottles next to my bed (empty).

I have no idea what time it is.

'We'll talk about this in the morning,' she says.

So it's not morning. Evening? Night? I can't tell.

Her voice is hard. Strict principal voice. I imagine her sticking me in detention for the rest of my time in St Agnes's.

Dad comes in later. 'Are you asleep?'

I stay silent. Still.

'I don't know what you're doing,' he says wearily.

It occurs to me to run away. To escape all of this. Parents who only step in for certain things but not others. Parents who close their eyes when it matters and open them when it suits them. Friends who are too caught up in their own identity crises to notice anything about you. Boys who will do anything just to get into bed with you. Boys who take drunk girls home to bed with them without thinking about how drunk they might be.

But I have no money and nowhere to go and this is my life. This is my prison. This.

Session one

The room: clean, pale green walls, framed degrees, bookshelves with titles about mindfulness and eating disorders and depression and schizophrenia. The therapist: Sheila Delaney, grey-haired, bright-eyed, wearing a bright-purple blouse and red skirt. Dangly earrings. Yellow A4 pad on lap. The client: Lauren Carroll, sulky, teenage, still in hideous maroon school uniform as she has come straight from the magical wonderland that is St Agnes's.

Sheila: 'Hello, Lauren, you're very welcome.'

Me: 'Hi.'

Sheila: 'Now, let me tell you a little bit about myself before we start, all right? Is this your first time in counselling?'

Me: 'Sort of.'

Sheila (nodding): 'Okay. Do you want to tell me a bit more about that?'

Me: 'Nope.'

Sheila (irritatingly calm): 'All right.' (Cue history as a nurse, then counsellor, including some do-gooder assignments in deprived parts of the world.) 'Now, do you want to tell me about why you're here?'

Me: 'My parents are making me.'

Sheila (smiling, like this is not the first time she's heard this): 'Okay. Why are they making you?'

Me: 'Didn't they tell you?'

Sheila: 'I want to hear what you think.'

Me: 'You're evading the question.' (Thinking: aren't you the one supposed to be saying that to *me*?)

Sheila: 'Lauren. I'm here for you to talk to. I'm not going to report back to your parents, unless . . .'

Me: 'Unless I say something that might put me or someone else at risk.' (Thank you, internet. Couldn't we just do this entirely online, with a virtual counsellor – a robot spouting out the clichés? It'd be cheaper and I could do it from bed. In pyjamas. With a drink in hand.)

Sheila: 'Exactly.'

Me: 'Define "risk".'

Sheila: 'Well, say for example, if I was worried – if I had a reasonable belief that you might injure yourself in some way. Then I'd be obliged to inform your parents, or even the police.'

Me: 'Define "injure myself".'

Sheila (leaning in, looking serious): 'Lauren, are you thinking about hurting yourself?'

Me: 'I'm just curious. What kind of things do you mean?'

Sheila: 'It wouldn't be appropriate for me to go into too much detail here.'

Me: 'What? Come on, tell me, I can take it. Suicide? Cutting? Burning?' (Trying to think of other ominous things here.)

Sheila: 'Those kinds of behaviours, yes. Or substance abuse.'

Me: 'Like alcohol or drugs.'

Sheila (warming to her topic): 'Exactly. Alcohol's a big one, of course, especially in this country. A lot of people feel that because it's legal, it's not a problem. And then there's drugs – and I don't just mean things like cocaine or heroin, the things you see on the news. We see a lot of prescription drug abuse as well. That'd be people taking drugs that they're not supposed to, even though they can be prescribed legally by a doctor . . .'

Me: 'Or maybe the drugs aren't legal here but are somewhere else.' (This is supposed to be a hint, Sheila.)

Sheila: 'Exactly. It's a big problem, Lauren. I hope it's something you never have any experience with.'

Me: 'Me too. Especially since you'd have to tell on me to my parents and the police.'

Sheila: 'Have you taken anything –'

Me (posh private-school-bitch voice): 'Goodness, no, I wouldn't dream of it.'

Sheila: 'I've a responsibility to anyone who comes into this office, Lauren. I don't want you to feel as though anyone will be "telling" on you just for the sake of it. In the very extreme circumstances where we might need to break our usual confidentiality, it's for your own good.'

Me: 'Sure.'

(Silence)

Sheila: 'Would you like to tell me what you're thinking about now?'

Me: 'Not really.' (That you should have guessed. That you should have figured it out. That's what I'm thinking. But I bet you don't want to know that, really, do you?)

Session two

The time: two days later. The room: unchanged. The therapist: white blouse, grey skirt, different set of dangly earrings. The client: worn out from the day at school.

Sheila: 'It's lovely to see you again, Lauren. Welcome.'

Me: 'How often do you see most people?'

Sheila: 'It all depends. Sometimes once a week, maybe once a fortnight, others as they need it. Everyone's different.'

Me: 'But would you agree with me that my parents insisting I come here twice a week is excessive?'

Sheila: 'Everyone's different. Let's give it a go for the moment and see how it works.'

Me: 'Whatever.'

Sheila: 'How was school today?' (Is she actually an aunt? How's school going? Look how tall you've grown!)

Me: 'Fine.'

Sheila: 'Anything interesting happen? Anything you'd like to discuss?'

Me: 'Not really.' (Pause.) 'We had to do this group presentation in English.'

Sheila: 'How did that go?'

Me (shrugging): 'Fine.'

Sheila: 'Do you get nervous, giving presentations?'

Me: 'Nah, not really. I love it.'

Sheila (surprised): 'Really?'

Me: 'Yeah.'

Sheila: 'Well, isn't that brilliant for you! So many people are terrified altogether of public speaking. Isn't it great that you enjoy it?'

Me: 'I suppose.'

Sheila: 'And what did you do your presentation about?'

Me: (gives a simplified explanation that omits Ann-Marie and Evan from the narrative entirely)

Sheila: 'That's very interesting, isn't it? We should all be looking more closely at the telly we watch, to make sure we're not just taking what it says for granted.'

Me: 'Yeah. I mean, there was one group and they looked at how TV programmes represented, um, medical procedures. My friend Tara talked about how – did you ever watch *House of Cards*? Not the old one, the Netflix one – and they have this whole bit with one of the characters where . . . oh, never mind, it's stupid, we're going off topic here.'

Sheila: 'I watched the old one all right. I read the books too. You know the first book had a completely different ending to the TV programme? And then the second book pretended that didn't happen, because the TV version was so popular.'

Me: 'Oh, really? That's so weird.'

Sheila: 'I must watch the new one. Is it only on the computer or are they showing it on any of the channels?'

Me: 'Um . . . I don't know. I think you can get it on DVD though.'

Sheila: 'I must do that, so. I love a good box-set.'

Me: 'It's good, yeah. My dad loves it.'

Sheila: 'And what was the thing you were saying about medical procedures? Will I get cross with them getting things wrong? I get very cross watching medical dramas sometimes, I drive everyone bananas.'

Me: 'I see what you're doing here.' (I am not an idiot.)

Sheila: 'Well, Lauren, you're a smart girl. Go on. Tell me what you need to tell me.' (She sits back in her chair, her hands folded in her lap.)

Me: 'There's this bit where one of the characters can't get pregnant and her doctor says it's because she's had three abortions. Which is *complete* bullshit unless they were performed in, like, some dodgy back-alley clinic, which they never talk about, they just act like it's totally normal to lie to audiences and scare them and make it sound like having an abortion will screw up your chances at ever having kids again. I mean, it's a *doctor* who tells her this.'

Sheila: 'You sound very angry about this.'

Me: 'Well, Sheila, you're a smart woman. Tell me why *you* think I might be angry about this.'

Sheila: 'Have you had an abortion?'

Me: (pause) 'Yes.'

Sheila: 'Okay. Let's talk about that.'

Me: 'I had an abortion.' (Pause) 'Sorry, it's weird, I've never said it out loud before. Are you going to turn me over to the cops or tell my parents or something?'

Sheila: 'Unless there's any medical risk, there's no need to break confidentiality. We can talk about that, but I'm also going to refer you to a clinic that does free post-abortion check-ups.'

Me: 'Okay.'

Sheila: 'They also offer counselling, which would specialise in the feelings women might have after a termination . . . You can use that to support the work we're doing here, if you like. It's up to you.'

Me: 'I'm pretty sure I'm okay physically. But, like, yeah. A check-up would be good.'

Sheila: 'And emotionally?'

Me: 'I don't know.' (I do know. I'm just scared to say it. Scared of seeming like a monster.)

Sheila: 'Okay. We can come back to this.'

Me: 'You're wearing a cross.'

Sheila: 'I am indeed. Are you spiritual at all?'

Me: 'No.' (pause) 'Is that going to be a problem?'

Sheila: 'Not at all. I don't see myself being put on this earth as here to judge. I'm here to help people.'

Me: 'Put on this earth by . . . God?'

Sheila (shrugging): 'That's my take on it. It doesn't have to be yours.'

Me: 'Holy shit, you're a nun.'

Sheila: 'I am. I trained with . . .'

Me: 'Are you even *allowed* to wear nice jewellery if you're a nun?'

Sheila: 'We all have our little weaknesses, don't we?'

Hysterical

I leave Sheila's office wondering if there are hidden cameras somewhere and fighting the urge to let out a hysterical giggle. It's just too ridiculous. My therapist is a nun. Of course. Of course she is.

My do-gooder-nun-therapist knows I had an abortion – which also means I had sex! Almost as bad! – and didn't even say that she'd pray for my soul. Which I suppose is something.

Sitting in the reception area is a face I know but it takes a minute for my brain to catch up. Marc. Our eyes meet.

The hysteria dissipates. Now it's just panic. But I see it on his face too. This is a weird place to see someone that you know.

I offer up a tiny smile. A sheepish one. Here we are.

A nod in return. Here we are. Our secret.

Session three

The time: the following week. The room: a little bit more sunlight. (Sister) Sheila: yellow blouse with embroidered daisies, forest-green skirt, dangly duck-shaped earrings. Me: out of school uniform, on account of it being the mid-term break. Floaty dress with cardigan over it, sort of girly-girl meets old-maiden-trying-to-cover-everything-up.

Sheila: 'Hello, Lauren, you're very welcome.'

Me: 'My mum thinks I'm an alcoholic.'

Sheila: 'Why do you say that?'

Me: 'She dropped me off and said something about how it must be working if I've stopped drinking. Which, like . . . if she really thought that, wouldn't she have sent me off to rehab somewhere?' (Imagining: sitting around in a circle, 'Hi, my name is Lauren and I'm an alcoholic.' Other people getting up and telling their stories. Art therapy. Rocking back and forth in a chair talking about your childhood. Getting sobriety chips. How much of this is potentially realistic and how much is from TV, Lauren? Remember, TV lies.)

Sheila: 'Do you feel as though you should be in a rehab programme?'

Me: 'No, I just . . .' (struggling for words) 'It just feels like it should be more drastic than this. I used to think counselling was this big important thing that sorts everything out for you, but it's just talking.'

Sheila: 'Sometimes we need to talk.' (Pauses) 'I'm going to give you a survey about alcohol use, is that all right?'

Me: 'Okay.'

(Paper handed over. Statements read. Things circled. Paper handed back.)

Sheila: (says things about binge drinking and women and units and liver damage)

Me: 'Everyone does it, come on. You're making it sound so dramatic.'

Sheila: (gives a speech about how blackouts are not normal)

Me: 'It happens to everyone who drinks, sometimes.'

Sheila: 'No, Lauren, it doesn't.'

Session four

The time: still on mid-term break. Sheila's outfit today: floral patterned dress with a cardigan, dangly flower-shaped earrings. Mine: jeans and long-sleeved T-shirt with quotes from TV all over it.

Sheila (after usual welcomes): 'Did you get a chance to look at that book I lent you?'

Me (rooting it out of bag): 'Yep. Finished it.'

Sheila: 'You're a quick reader.'

Me: 'It's mid-term, it's not like I've homework to do. Actually, I'm in TY, it's not like I ever have much homework to do.'

Sheila: 'Are you bored in school?'

Me: 'Isn't that the point? Either you're studying for exams and you're stressed or you're not and you're bored.'

Sheila: 'That's a rather grim take on our educational system.'

Me: 'It's a pretty grim system.'

Sheila: 'Do you get on well in school?'

Me: 'I get on okay. Not great.'

Sheila: 'You strike me as very clever.'

Me: 'I'm not. Not really. My friend – an old friend of mine – he's really smart.'

Sheila: 'Sometimes we find it hard to have the same confidence that men do, Lauren.'

Me: (debates explaining, decides it's too complicated) 'So this book.'

Sheila: 'What did you make of it?'

Me: 'Like, she starts drinking really young and then keeps going, of *course* she has a problem. But it doesn't look at why she does it; it's not like anything's happened to her. There's a difference between getting drunk when your life is shit and just getting drunk because.'

Sheila: 'Are you sure about that?'

Me: 'Yeah, isn't it obvious?'

Sheila: 'When was the first time you got drunk?'

Me: 'I don't know. A bit over a year ago, maybe?'

Sheila: 'Why were you drinking?'

Me: 'Because . . . everyone else was. Ugh, look, I know that sounds stupid, it wasn't a *peer pressure* thing. It was a party and there was alcohol.'

Sheila: 'But you were underage.'

Me: 'Is this another thing where you have to call the police in?'

Sheila: 'I'm just making the point. Were you the youngest there? Were there older people there?'

Me: 'Um . . . not that much older. I guess there were a couple of people who were actually eighteen, they were the oldest.'

Sheila: 'There's a big gap between fifteen and eighteen.'

Me: 'Yeah. I mean, it depends on the individual, I guess.'

Sheila: 'Did anything happen . . .'

Me: 'Let me save you some time. No creepy older guy did

250

anything to me, okay? I'm not scarred for life from that.'

Sheila (mildly): 'Okay. So, the first time you got drunk, it was social – is that fair to say? Tell me about the second time.'

Me: 'I don't know, I don't remember.'

Sheila (leaning forward in that therapist way): 'Did it become a pattern?'

Me: 'You say it like it's so *sinister*. Teenagers drink, Sheila.'

Sheila: 'I know they do. And I worry about them. But just because a lot of young people are drinking, and drinking to excess, doesn't mean that it's healthy. And I don't think you –' (tapping survey from last session, on her clipboard) 'have a healthy relationship with alcohol.'

Me: 'I can't actually believe we're talking about this and not the fucked-up-ness of this country.'

Sheila: 'Do you mean the attitudes towards alcohol?'

Me: 'I mean . . . I mean everything. But. Oh, you know what I mean. Why do I have to say it?'

Sheila: 'Lauren, I might be able to guess what you mean, but it's always more effective if someone actually articulates what they're thinking.'

Me: 'I had an abortion.'

Sheila: 'Have you decided how you feel about that?'

Me: 'I want to set this fucking country on fire.'

Sheila: 'I'll put down "angry", shall I?'

251

Blackout

I have to know. If I can. I have to. Sheila's making the world tilt and there's something ready to crack, some hard truth looming behind the curtain.

I turn on my laptop, open up Facebook. Start clicking. Dublin is a village. I know this. Stay online long enough and you can find anyone. And I do, the familiar face turning up in the right-hand column. Familiar only because I keep staring at the photos from that night. 'Add friend,' I click. Heart racing.

A few minutes later: friend request accepted. And a message.

Mike: *Hey Lauren, are u ok?*

Mike: *Been wondering if u were since u left.*

Me: *Yeah, just a bit morto.*

Me: *Actually a lot morto.*

Mike: *No worries, we've all been there! :)*

Me: *Haha not this bad. Don't remember anything.*

Me: *Ugh, am such a disaster. :(*

Mike: *U were out of it alright!*

Mike: *U took all ur clothes off & kept saying u needed to have sex with some1!!*

Me: *DYING.*

Mike: *I had to go sleep in guest room!!*
Me: *What, you didn't seduce me??*
Mike: *Meant 2 but u were 2 out of it.*
Mike: *Wouldn't mind trying again 2 b honest!!*
Me: *We'll see . . .*
Me: *Thanks for being a decent guy!*
Mike: *haha!*
Mike: *seriously let me know.*

Shaking.

So much shaking.

Relief but also fear of the maybe. The kind of fear you can only acknowledge when you know you're safe.

I think of the book Sheila lent to me. The American woman who had loads of blackouts. Sex she didn't remember. Maybe didn't even happen but maybe it did and she didn't know. She never knew.

This is my body and I want to know. Always. I tighten my arms around myself. Pull my knees up to my chest. Me. Me. Me.

Sheila thinks I am *abusing alcohol.*

Ellie asking me, was I drunk. *Ellie.*

Messages I can't remember typing.

Things I can't remember happening.

(It's not a big deal.)

(Everyone my age drinks.)

(Blackouts aren't normal.)

(I don't want to think about this.)

Inspiration

'You've got to do something else with those feelings,' she says at the end of our next session. 'Drowning them isn't healthy.'

'I'm not drowning them,' I say irritably. No alcohol for Lauren these days. Go me. Can I have a gold star instead of a lecture, please?

'Do you think you're processing them?'

'No,' I say, sulkily. I know I sound like a kid. But I don't know what else to say. I always thought counselling was supposed to fix you. To leave you feeling better rather than worse.

'Well, that's something for us to look at over the next couple of weeks. I'd like you to think about how you might express your emotions in a healthier way.'

'Sure. Whatever.' I stomp back out to the reception area of the counselling centre. And there he is again. Marc.

'Hi,' I say. It's only slightly awkward.

'Hi.'

I pause, and then it bursts out of me. I need to know if other people get annoyed by their therapists. 'Are you seeing Sheila?' I ask.

He shakes his head. 'Derek.' He nods towards one of the other doors. 'Inspirational.'

It takes me a moment to realise he's being sarcastic. 'That bad, huh?'

'If you're going through hell,' Marc intones, 'keep going.'

'Oh, that's special.'

Marc nods. Offers up a smile. 'Yeah. Real helpful when you're suicidal, like.'

I freeze. 'Are you?'

'I was.' He shrugs.

My *heart.* 'Oh, pet,' I say.

'It's okay. Talking through it, all that shit. *Processing* the feelings.'

My eyes are stupidly full. 'I'm so sorry.'

'Hey, hey, I didn't mean to upset you –'

I wave him off. 'No, it's fine, I just – I had no idea. I kinda forgot that Q Club is where –'

I can't finish the sentence but he knows what I mean.

'Yeah,' he says.

'I get that too,' I say quickly, before I can lose my nerve. 'The *processing* stuff. I don't have a fucking clue.'

'You know what you *should* try, though?' Marc says, all serious.

'What?'

'Meditation.'

'Fuck. Right. Off.'

We crack up, and then Inspirational Derek sticks his head around the door to call Marc in for his appointment. I attempt an awkward friendly punch-in-the-shoulder move, which is

255

kindly reciprocated, and then sit in reception for another few minutes, waiting for my legs to stop trembling.

Something's cracked open in me. Marc. Marc is a human with his own inner life who goes to counselling too. Not just some evil Steph stealer/influencer/whatever. Just someone sad. Someone hurting.

But also someone you might turn to if you were hurting too, in a way that your best friend couldn't understand.

Rosemary's face flashes in front of my eyes, then. Shared experiences count. I get it. I do.

I breathe in. And out. And then I pick up my phone.

Temptation

There is beer in the fridge and my parents are out.

There is beer in the fridge and I know I had counselling just yesterday, which was prompted by overindulging in such things but.

I want it.

I want to slip into fuzzy-edged reality. Where I am not the girl fighting with her best friend. Where I am not the girl who spent her Christmas money on a secret abortion in another country. Where everything is easier.

Is that 'abusing alcohol', Sheila, to want something that will make the crappy world less crappy?

And do I care?

I am on the stairs when there's a click at the front door. Dad's home.

(But I *wanted* . . .)

That tilt of the world happens again, where it seems like maybe it is a *problem*.

I hide under my duvet, waiting for sleep.

The Boy Friend

'You're coming along great!' Ms Lynch says encouragingly at our next rehearsal. These are becoming more polished. Sort of. Everyone knows the words, the moves, except for one of the Perfect Young Ladies with a small speaking role who keeps bursting into (unscripted) giggles. I sense, rather than witness, Evan's eye-rolling.

A straight run-through of Act One today. I am more aware than ever of how wrong 'The Boy Friend' is for me, and for Evan. Our eyes meet – he got the message, he's going to meet me after this – and lift to the heavens. We're playing the wrong parts here, and it's entirely to do with how we look and the shape of our bodies and it feels so stupidly reductive I want to scream.

But then again, I often have this feeling within the walls of St Agnes's.

When we're finished, Mrs O'Connor lists all the things we need to work on and Ms Lynch chimes in with what we're doing well. Normally this double-act would amuse me but my guts are all knotted up and I just want to get out of here.

'Okay,' Evan says as soon I get to the school gates. 'What is it?'

I can't. This is too big for words.

'I,' I start.

I should have practised in front of the mirror. Made notes. Because what comes out of my mouth is the most pathetic thing ever. 'Do you even *remember* that we slept together?'

Evan stares at me. 'Yeah.'

'Okay.' I look at my feet. 'Because we haven't talked about it.'

'Is that what – Laur, it was stupid, it freaked me out . . .'

'I know!' My voice comes out louder than I anticipate. 'I know. Icky girl-bodies freak you out, I get it. I freak you out. I fucking *get it.*'

Evan looks around, and I realise there are a few other students drifting out of school eyeing us up with great interest.

'Let's go –' we say in unison.

When we settle down in a cafe down the road, the momentum's lost. We order hot chocolate and sit awkwardly for a moment. Then Evan says, '*It* freaked me out. Not you. I mean, you're . . .'

I wait.

'. . . my best friend,' he finishes, and something inside me clenches.

'Best friend' shouldn't feel like second place, but right now it does.

'Okay,' I say. 'It was just, timing-wise . . . it felt like seeing me naked was . . .'

'What, like it *turned* me?' Evan says incredulously.

'No. Yeah. Kind of. I know, it's stupid.'

'Yeah.' I'm expecting a lecture, but instead he goes, 'I didn't even think about how you'd take it. I just thought you were being, you know –'

'Horrible transphobic bitch lady,' I supply.

He nods. 'Yeah. Look, Laur, this isn't about you.'

'I know. I get that. Your stuff – that's your story. And I thought you and Marc were – like, ugh, I don't know.'

'We're friends,' he says. And then, like it's obvious, 'Because I like *girls*, Laur.'

'Yeah, well, as far as I was concerned you *were* one, okay? I mean, what was I supposed to –' I stop. 'This isn't about that.'

'Okay. So what's it about? You've been weird. And really – angry.'

Yeah. Yeah, I am. 'Can I tell you a thing about the crapness of female biology without you thinking it means I don't get you're a boy or Ellie's a girl?' I pause. 'I mean, do you care? Is this a thing we can't talk about any more?'

'Of course I *care*.'

'It's just . . . Look, I *get* it, people go through these stages where everything's about their own stuff, so if you're there, that's okay. I'll shut up about mine.'

Evan offers up a little smile. 'Did Ellie give you the speech?'

'Yeah,' I say sheepishly.

'Me too.'

'What? Why?'

'Ah, you know what she's like. She's been worried about you. She said, basically, *it's really hard but it doesn't mean everything's about you either.*'

'Oh,' I say in a tiny voice. Ellie's not taking sides. Ellie still cares. I press my right hand hard against my mouth to try to stop the verge-of-tears sensations.

'Fuck. Laur, what's up? What *happened*?'

I take a slurp of hot chocolate to try to make everything better. 'Did you follow that, um, news thing,' I start, but can't get any further.

Evan frowns. 'What thing?'

I fish my phone out from my pocket. The article, that first one, is saved on it. I open it up, pass the phone over.

Evan takes the phone and stares at the screen, looking confused. 'Laur –'

'Don't judge me,' I say, already feeling the panic. This is it.

'It's not loading, you eejit,' Evan says, handing the phone back to me with a blank white screen.

'Oh.'

And then we're laughing, snorting ugly laughs. (It's so much easier, kinder, to see people face-to-face, not through screens.) I connect to the cafe's wifi, let the thing load. Hand it back feeling already lighter. 'There.'

Evan's always been able to read super-quickly. There's concentration, but his face stays the same. Scroll down a bit more. Read. A bit more. Read. And then. 'That's your voice,' he says softly. The quote at the end.

'Yeah.'

'Are you still – did you –'

'Got the boat. Well. Ryanair flight.'

'Was, what's-his-face, was Justin okay with it? Did he go with you?'

The laugh that spurts out of me surprises us both. 'Uh, no. He doesn't know. It's okay. He's an idiot.'

'Oh. Okay. Well, at least your mum's decent.'

'She doesn't know.'

Evan stares at me. 'Lauren Carroll. You are not fucking telling me you did this all by yourself.' His voice gets louder. 'You *come* to me with this shit, okay?'

'We weren't even talking,' I protest.

'Some things are bigger than not-talking!' He brushes a hand over his eyes. 'Okay. I'm going to hug you now, and it's going to be a crap hug because you're taller than me and you need a big bear-hug, but it's the best I got, okay?'

'Okay,' I say, and he gets out of his seat and hugs me from behind, tight as anything. I breathe in a mix of scents: how Steph used to smell, how Evan smells now. I breathe in. I can't remember the last time I felt this safe – without alcohol sloshing through my veins, I mean. 'Best friend' status edges its way closer to the top.

'I'm here for you. No matter what. Okay?' Evan says into my ear.

I nod. And when he finally lets go I say, 'Yeah, you were right. That was a crap hug.'

Poet

Inspired by YouTube spoken word performed by beautiful artsy girls, I write a poem. It has metaphors and similes and dramatic pauses. It is about blood and alcohol. Pain and pleasure. Body and soul.

I practise it in front of the mirror, trying to speak the way the girls in the videos do. John's done spoken word, I remember, although his is of the funnier variety. Amp up the camp and go for the laughs. Easier to get away with that as a guy.

I intone the words solemnly, record myself, and then play it back.

Yes. Yes. Absolutely. This poem is completely, unequivocally, shit.

Sheila's other suggestion for *expressing my feelings* was to draw, but I have no idea where to begin. I remember Fee's elephant, smile a little.

Okay. Research. The *Hamilton* soundtrack is on while I click and search. An episode of that weird *BoJack Horseman* cartoon turns up. Then there's a few reviews of an Irish musical about contraceptives. I find some fairly tasteless jokes ('What's red and crawls up your leg?' 'A homesick abortion!') and some decent ones. Articles about that *House of Cards* episode Tara talked about in her presentation. A lot of weird artwork involving menstrual blood. An American legal drama from about a decade ago that had an episode called 'Roe v Wade: the musical!' but is not actually a musical. More weird menstrual-blood art (I should probably find it empowering and not gross, but . . .).

There's a romantic comedy with an abortion in it. Everyday ordinary rom-com except with this thing that I suddenly realise I've never seen handled in this way before. I watch the girl curl up on the couch afterwards and her boyfriend minding her and I have a moment of aching before reminding myself that in that situation, Justin would probably have asked me for a blow-job.

Hamilton finishes up and I click over to *Avenue Q*. Excitement zig-zags through my veins in a way I haven't felt since – since auditioning, I guess. I know how to tell my story. I know the thing I need to make.

Opening night

Okay, let's be realistic here. My musical about abortion in Ireland is not the sort of thing you can write in a week. But I've looked into different programmes and camps for this summer and I've found a couple Mum and Dad might be willing to send me to. Places that sound sufficiently educational enough to please them but practical enough to be a good starting point for me.

In the meantime, it's opening night of *The Boy Friend*. The musical to make all other musicals look competent. In the changing rooms, I am in my cream jumper and trousers, half tempted to stuff a sock down there for verisimilitude (Ms Lynch used the word last week in class and I have been trying it out ever since). How realistically can I portray a (cis, yes, obviously) man if I am not managing his genitalia?

I'm nervous in that good way before a performance: shaky but also excited.

Curtain up. Hortense, the maid, is on stage first. When the schoolgirls crowd in, all giggly and silly, she asks in an over-the-top French accent if *zey have forgozzen who zey are*.

265

Cue 'Perfect Young Ladies', in their navy and white dresses and high heels.

Then they're swooning over Imelda-as-Polly's costume idea for the ball, and Imelda launches into the opening of 'The Boy Friend'. Her voice is thin and wobbly, which some people might attribute to nerves. In fact, it sounds exactly as it has the whole way through rehearsals.

The other girls join in, and then along we come – the 'boys'. Some in straw hats, others with hair pulled back and tucked away. A few girls have even drawn moustaches on their faces. I realise that Katie, in front of me, has actually given herself cat whiskers, and I bite back a smile.

We are danced around like hat racks and then go off stage again. Imelda-as-Polly fakes having a boyfriend and Fee-as-Madame-Dubonnet says 'poor little rich girl' – one of those lines that should elicit a laugh from the audience but doesn't. I wonder how many of them are here just to support their kids and are barely paying attention to what's actually happening on the stage.

Tara's up next, for Maisie and Bobby's duet. I can't see the dancing but the singing sounds great. The girl playing Bobby is delivering a passable baritone and Tara – well, she's fabulous, and I'm not just saying that because she's my friend or because she's agreed to my fiendish little scheme without hesitation. For the first time, it occurs to me that even if Mrs O'Connor didn't have it in for me, Tara would still have been the better choice for the part.

Watch me grow as a person! Isn't it amazing what twice-weekly (okay, we're down to weekly, now) counselling with a jewellery-addicted nun will do for you?

Cue more falling-in-love sequences: Madame Dubonnet meets Polly's father, Percival Browne, and realises he's an 'old friend', if you know what I mean. The girl playing Percy used to be my science partner back in first year. The class-clown type, which means she's not quite a fit for the role of a stuffy older man. I feel bad for Fee. Then Ann-Marie, as Tony, comes along and she and Imelda do a duet, having fallen in love at first sight.

Act Two. The adrenaline increases. A different set of girls from the Perfect Young Ladies dance in old-fashioned swimming costumes to 'Sur La Plage' and we meet Tony's parents (who are rich! So he is an acceptable suitor for Polly after all!). Tony and Polly continue planning their future together, a sort of idealised version of poverty. They almost kiss, and probably do in the real script, but we couldn't possibly have that on stage here.

For a second I imagine Ann-Marie and Imelda hooking up and it is both hilarious and deeply disturbing.

Following some casual anti-French racism, which I've been finding weirdly familiar and only recently realised it's because it's the same sort of stuff you get in Enid Blyton's school stories, Madame Dubonnet and Percy are up again.

I can hardly breathe.

We're really going to do this.

Maisie comes on stage, fretful. In rehearsals she's skipped in merrily. Beside me, someone's whispering, 'Is she okay?'

Madame Dubonnet comes back on stage.

Whispers get more intense. This is not in the script.

'Maizee, what is ze matter? You look so pale!'

'Oh, Madame Dubonnet,' Maisie sighs. 'I'm afraid I've got myself into a bit of a scrape.'

'*Zut alors!* Wazzever can zis be?'

'It's – it's – oh, I don't know quite how to put it, Madame!' Tara's posh British schoolgirl accent never falters. My heart bursts with pride.

'What the hell are they doing?' murmurs Katie, to my left. Everyone backstage is listening intently, with bewildered expressions on their faces. Everyone except me, who's pulling off her jumper and undoing her tight plait while everyone else is distracted.

'Maizee, is it – are you in ze family way? Up ze pole? Bun in ze oven?'

'Oh, Madame, it's *much* worse than that. I'm pregnant!'

The audience cracks up and I can't help feel a little rush. Okay, a big rush.

'Maizee! Zis is quite ze shock.'

'I know, Madame. I'm not ready for a baby. I'm not even ready to settle down. I want to – keep my options open, I suppose.'

'Well, my dear child, zis is what you shall do!'

'Oh, but Madame –'

'Zis is France, Maizee! We are ceevilised! We do not want you to have *un bébé* if zis is not your weesh.'

'Oh, Madame!' A pause as they hug. 'I thought – oh, I was so scared.'

'But of course, Maizee! I have not forgozzen zat your grandmuzzer was from Ireland. Zey are not so civilised. But you must not hold zat against them, *ma petite*. Zey make excellent whiskey.'

More laughter, though it is a little gaspy. A little as though they can't quite believe it.

I can't quite either.

'Oh, Madame, *thank* you!'

I emerge on stage. Without the heavy jumper hiding my breasts, and with my hair down, I am very clearly a girl. 'Madame Dubonnet, Mr Browne is looking for you,' I say politely.

'But what is zees?' Madame Dubonnet waves a hand in my direction. 'I cannot tell whezzer you are *une femme* or *un homme*!'

'Don't be silly, Madame Dubonnet,' Maisie pipes up. 'This is clearly a . . .' She starts to mouth 'boy', then changes to 'girl', then just looks blank.

Another burst of laughter from the audience.

'Oh, who cares!' Maisie says cheerfully. 'Let's go for a walk, you darling thing. Have a jolly time with Mr Browne, Madame!'

Maisie and I exit stage left, Madame Dubonnet stage right.

Many many bewildered faces.

'You were incredible,' I whisper to Tara.

She hugs me, then skips back out on stage again for her real entrance – skipping along and getting ready for 'Safety in Numbers'.

'What the fuck?' screeches Ann-Marie, suddenly in my face. 'What are you playing at, Lauren Carroll?'

I am about to say something when Katie steps in. 'Leave her alone.'

'This is not acceptable,' Ann-Marie insists. Still far too close to me than is comfortable. I nudge her away.

'That was *mad*,' Gillian from my maths class says, admiringly.

I offer up a smile, as I start plaiting my hair again.

'Leave it,' Katie says suddenly.

Gillian pulls her jumper over her head. Erica who I've never said two words to in my life pulls out a lipstick and offers it around.

'What are you *doing*?' Ann-Marie shrieks. 'I'm reporting you all for this. It's *so* disrespectful.'

'Oh, shut up,' Gillian says.

When we march out as the gentlemen chorus for 'Safety in Numbers', five of the girls in trousers have their hair loosened, their bosom-hiding jumpers removed, and reddened lips. We do everything we're supposed to, everything we rehearsed. We are just clearly girls while doing it.

By the time Imelda and Ann-Marie are out on stage again, they are shaking with fury. And it's fair to say that most of the year think it's a stupid prank, that we've just wasted time or messed things up. But there's enough – the five lipsticked 'boys', Fee, Tara, and a few others coming over to offer up impressed noises – to cancel that out.

The third act goes according to plan – and would have even without Mrs O'Connor storming backstage and hissing at me, but I'm untouchable tonight – and yet it has somehow more energy to it than it did before. The audience are more tuned in. They laugh at the bits that are supposed to be funny but have never felt it in rehearsals. It's like messing with it has given the show an extra dimension – maybe it's not as tongue-in-cheek for a modern audience as it might have been all those decades ago. But by pointing out that it's a school play populated entirely by teenage girls, we've made it meta.

These are the thoughts I have as we go out on stage for the finale. Grand thoughts. Proud thoughts. Like maybe this is actually how you *should* do old-school musicals: a tiny bit of fourth-wall breaking and make it all so much more meaningful for the audience.

Then my mother, in an elegant grey suit, comes on stage to do the thank-yous and I come back down to Earth. 'Can we please have a warm round of applause to our magnificent co-directors, Carmel O'Connor and Elaine Lynch . . .'

My mother.

It's not like I forgot she existed, I just . . . didn't quite realise this was going to have to happen so soon.

Daughter

'I presume you're not going to pull this stunt again tomorrow night,' Mum says.

We're in the car. Still at school, in the car park, not moving. I've changed out of my costume and am back in jeans and a hoodie.

'Nope. Just tonight.'

'Good.' She sighs. 'Everyone in your year put a huge amount of work into that show, Lauren. It's not fair on them to use it for your own – agenda.'

I feel slightly guilty then. I know not everyone put a lot of effort in. For a lot of people it was just something we had to do. But for people like Ann-Marie and Imelda – okay, I'm not a good enough person to feel sorry for them. For *other* people, who worked hard, it's not fair. Opening night is a big deal. But there's two more shows. They can have them.

'The thing you need to do is write your own piece about all this,' Mum continues.

'I am,' I say, surprised. 'I mean, I will. Over the summer. I've some notes already.'

'Good.' She turns the key in the ignition and exits the car

park. 'Am I to take it that your trip to Liverpool wasn't for a friend?'

Here it comes. 'Yeah.'

'Okay,' she says, and swallows. 'Okay.'

I want to say that I'm sorry but it sticks in my mouth.

'Why didn't –' she starts, but I get in there first.

'Why didn't you *know*?' It comes out plaintive. I sound so young.

'What?'

'Mothers are supposed to –' I can't finish the sentence. The lump in my throat is a boulder.

A pause. 'To what? Be psychic?'

I still can't speak.

'What about fathers? Does your dad know?'

'No,' I whisper.

Oh God. What did I expect, really – some TV mother who would immediately know that I was keeping a secret from her, some kind of female intuition tipping her off, while good ol' Dad was allowed to be blissfully ignorant of it all? Both my parents work long hours at demanding jobs. And I told them nothing. Nothing at all.

I kept it all a secret while all the time hoping – expecting – a little extra patience from people. A little extra comfort.

'Have you talked to Sheila about it?' My mother is in business mode now, trying to figure things out as she navigates through traffic.

'Yep,' I say in a tiny voice.

'Okay. That's good. Have you been to a doctor?'

'Not since – no.'

'I'd like to get you checked out, just to make sure. And we should get you on the Pill.'

'It doesn't protect against infections,' I say. It is maybe not the right time to note this.

Because that's when my mother, who I have never seen cry ever in my entire *life*, starts gulping for air like a fish out of water and tears begin streaming down her face.

'I'm not angry with you,' she says after a few minutes.

We are parked outside our house now. The lights are on – Dad's home. He's coming to see the show on closing night. The less exciting version.

'You're just disappointed?' I guess.

She shakes her head. 'No.' And then, 'I'm disappointed in myself. You should have felt you could talk to me about this.'

Between the crying and this actual admission of a weakness I am starting to think my mother has been replaced by a dodgy impostor.

'Yeah, well,' I say, uselessly.

'Just the thought of you doing all that alone – I couldn't have done that at your age. I'm impressed. Seriously.'

This is not what I was expecting.

'And you don't – you didn't feel like you *had* to, did you? We could've sorted something out, if . . .'

This is the part where I should say something about how I thought long and hard about all available options and considered every single choice carefully. This is the part where I stick to acceptable rhetoric: never an easy decision. Always difficult. Always painful.

'I didn't want to be pregnant,' I say. And suddenly it is very simple. Because it is the truth. 'It was a really easy choice to make and I don't regret it. And maybe I will ten years from now but . . .' I shrug. Maybe I will. Maybe I will turn into one of those sad women who finds Jesus and spends their time sharing their stories of regret online. But I keep thinking of how scary it was to not have my body be my own. How relieved I was. (How utterly shit a dad Justin would have been.)

'You're some woman,' Mum says, and that's it, that's the point where I finally fling myself into my mother's arms for a long-awaited sobfest, for a long-awaited hug.

Encore

'Zey make excellent whiskey,' Fee, in character, says to Tara, and we cheer.

Tara delivers her line, and we cheer again.

(We're a little hyper.)

It's been a few weeks since the musical, but we enjoy running through this scene amongst ourselves. Because for the next bit, everyone likes taking turns. Ellie slinks in this time. It's the first time I've seen her in a dress.

(Am I allowed to be envious of how she looks more elegant in it than I ever could?)

'I cannot tell whezzer you are *une femme* or *un homme*!' Fee declares. She gets such a kick out of getting to keep doing her French accent. 'Are you perhaps one of zees modern – how do zey say – genderqueers?'

We all crack up.

'I can be whatever you want me to be, Madame,' Ellie says, breathily.

'Ooh la la!' Fee goes along with it.

They fake-make-out while the rest of us applaud.

I didn't find out until the next day that Ellie was there on opening night. We cried at each other and then I told her I was in counselling and she was *thrilled*.

Sometimes we swap notes on therapy-talk and Marc joins in. Mostly, though, Marc and I have the chats about hormones and how crazy they are. What it means to take one to become the boy you are inside. What it means to take a combination of another to control the crazy periods and threat of pregnancy that makes you hate being a girl. Everyone else starts making vomiting noises and cries of 'not again!' when we get on this topic, which I will allow is fair.

'Okay,' I say once the applause dies down, 'are we ready for our movie of joy?'

Movie night at my house is alcohol-free, but we have plenty of crisps and chocolate and takeaway pizza. Dad, always with an eye on cost, has already noted that it's better value to make up your own pizzas at home, but my eye is on taste.

'What's the movie?' Ronan, John's new boyfriend, asks. It's his first time meeting any of us. He's managed not to faint from nerves so far.

'*Legally Blonde*,' I say. 'It's a feminist masterpiece.'

'Oooh! Yay!' Tara claps her hands in delight.

'Isn't that the one where she's really ditzy?' Sandra asks.

'It's a feminist masterpiece,' Tara and I repeat.

To Sandra's credit, she laughs instead of getting huffy with us. She curls into Ellie's side, completely unbothered by what might look like a boy in a dress to an outsider. I need to remember that seeming like you fit in somewhere doesn't mean you really do. Or that you can't fit in somewhere else as well. There's no secret boyfriend. Just a hopeless devotion to Ellie. It's both endearing and sickening.

'We should watch the sequel as well,' Ronan says enthusiastically.

'Congratulations,' I say. 'You have passed the test. You may now go do naughty things to John.'

'Thanks, Laur,' John says, sticking his tongue out at me. 'Always good to have your permission.'

'All hail Lauren, queen of the gays,' Evan calls out.

'Evan, what did we say about respecting people's identities?' Ellie says, shaking a finger like a cross mammy. 'Lauren is not gay, she's – how are you putting it these days?'

'An equal-opportunities cuddle-slut,' I say.

'So, bi,' Katie says, just to be clear.

'Well,' Fee says, 'actually – ooh, I can do this one! – that's really reductive because it presumes . . . a binary concept of gender!'

We all cheer. Fee gets very excited about picking up bits of jargon and then being able to explain them. It's adorable.

Katie laughs. 'Okay. Whatever works for you, Laur. Some of us are just plain-and-simple gay.'

So, it turns out that my and Evan's assessment of Katie a couple of years ago as 'super-straight' was in fact super-inaccurate. She and Tara are kind of a thing. And it all started the night of the musical, when they had a mutual appreciation-fest that led to what I'm told was an 'intensely sexually charged atmosphere, totally lesbionic' (Tara's words).

'Lauren's complicated,' Ellie teases, and then comes over to give me a hug. 'You doing okay?' she whispers.

It is funny and also sort of inspiring to see what happens

when you actually tell people what's been going on in your life, instead of just expecting them to be psychic. I feel taken-care-of by my friends in a way I thought you needed a romantic (okay, sex) partner for.

'Yeah,' I say, hugging her back. 'Let's watch the movie!'

I try not to stare at Evan too much, as the super-girly opening credits roll. That night is still so vivid. Fingers. Eyes on mine. Breathlessness. Everything so intense like it was happening in slow motion or like new colours had been invented.

But that's my story of the night, and his is very different. And someday, someday that'll be okay.

I watch Reese Witherspoon as Elle Woods on the screen and I say, 'I'd kill to be that confident.'

The entire room cracks up.

'Yeah, imagine being confident enough to fuck with your school musical to get a point across,' Tara says.

'Or to let yourself be interviewed in *the actual newspaper* about that fake clinic place,' Fee adds.

After Mum and I told Dad and then we all told Brian and Liz (not that it was really any of their business, except I wanted to explain where exactly the money went to), I went back to the initial news stories about the clinic and read so many nasty comments about how the 'anonymous girl' was clearly completely invented (also nasty comments about various other things, ranging from calling all women sluts and bitches to rape threats for the journalist who went undercover) I contacted Susan Pollard and asked if it was worth putting my name to it. (I didn't name Justin. I don't know if he even realises.)

The Pro-Choice Alliance want me to give a speech at

some assembly they're holding, but I think someone like Rosemary would be better. It's too easy to dismiss a teenage girl. I already get enough hate-mail from the pro-lifers, not to mention well-intentioned messages about how I'm too young to understand what I did but they'll pray for me.

And anyway, I'd rather work on my musical.

'Yeah, you're such a wimp, Laur,' Evan says. Smiling at me.

'Oh, shut up,' I say, pleased.

'Yeah, yeah, we all love Lauren, but can we watch the movie?' Ellie says.

I give her the finger.

'That's so *unladylike*,' Tara says, pretending to be horrified.

I lean back on the couch, the corners of my mouth turning up. 'Damn right.'

Acknowledgements

First off, a quick note: I would love to say that the situations Lauren encounters in this book with regard to reproductive rights in Ireland are exaggerated for dramatic purposes. When I started writing this, my secret hope was that it would already be 'historical fiction' by the time it was published. As of spring 2017, however, it is still illegal to obtain an abortion in Ireland unless you are literally dying on a hospital bed, in which case a panel of doctors might agree to provide the procedure. If you're lucky. The figure given in the book of Irish women travelling abroad for abortions in a particular year is invented but falls within the typical range of women travelling annually in real life. The 'Baby Hope' scenario Lauren has nightmares about is a real case. Pregnancy crisis centres offering up blatant lies to vulnerable women are real. However, the names of organisations and campaigners on 'both sides' used in the novel are fictional and not intended to correspond directly with any real-life equivalent.

Useful texts if you're researching this topic (aside from newspaper articles, personal essays and, of course, Tumblr):

Katha Pollitt's *Pro* and Kitty Holland's *Savita*. For other topics touched on in the novel, the most useful books were Natasha Walters's *Living Dolls*, Arin Andrews's *Some Assembly Required*, and Sarah Hepola's *Blackout*.

Also: pop-culture references in the text! The movie then-Steph-now-Evan and Lauren watch is *But I'm A Cheerleader*; the relevant episode of *House of Cards* is the season 1 finale; the relevant episode of *BoJack Horseman* is season 3, episode 6; the Irish musical about contraceptives is Arthur Riordan & Bill Whelan's *The Train*; 'Roe v Wade: the musical!' is an episode of *Boston Legal*; the abortion-themed rom-com is *Obvious Child*.

Onto the thank-you section! I am very grateful to the Arts Council for their generous support (and validating-of-neurotic-writer-ego). My thanks also to the Tyrone Guthrie Centre at Annaghmakerrig, for a warm, creative space to embark on final edits.

Many thanks to: my fellow Banshees, Laura Jane Cassidy and Eimear Ryan, for indulging me in ramblings about this book before a single word was written. Deirdre Sullivan, for walks and writer-chats. E. R. Murray and Ruth Frances Long for the Room of Joy. Fiona Deverell and John Harris for insights and support on various chapters. Declan Hughes, Dave Lordan, Sarah Maria Griffin, Kerrie O'Brien and Sinead Gleeson for writerly bravery and confidence. YA bookclub (of wonder). Nicole, Fran & all at Big Smoke. The Dublin Random Penguins. Ali Brennan for